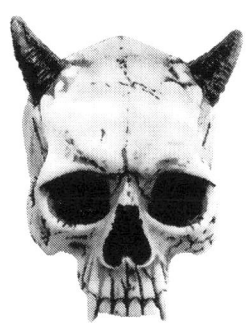

MAMA MIA

COPYRIGHT

Mama Mia

Copyright © 2018 by Marcus Blakeston.
All rights reserved.

This is a work of fiction. Names, characters, businesses, places, events, and incidents are the product of the author's imagination. Any resemblance to actual persons, living or dead, events, or places is entirely coincidental.

A slightly different version of this book was previously published as Biker Sluts versus Flying Saucers in 2015.

http://marcusblakeston.wordpress.com

marcus.blakeston@gmail.com

http://www.facebook.com/marcus.blakeston

ALSO AVAILABLE

Runaway

Punk Rock Nursing Home

Skinhead Away

Bare Knuckle Bitch

Meadowside

Punk Faction

INTRODUCTION

I don't remember how old I was the first time I watched the original George Pal version of War of the Worlds on TV, but it left a big impression on me. I'd never seen anything like it before. After that I made sure I watched every alien invasion film I could. My favourites were the black and white ones from the 1950s, with bug-eyed aliens determined to wipe humanity from the face of the planet. I'd act them out in the local woods, throwing sticks at imaginary flying saucers and hiding behind trees when anyone walked by who looked like they might be an alien in disguise. Sometimes I'd cough in their general direction, in the hope a simple germ I was immune to would wipe them out. But it never did. They took over anyway, and left me as one of the few people who knew the truth.

Years later, when I was 10, I found Peter Cave's Hells Angels book 'Chopper' in the remainder section at the local Woolworths. I was already reading the Richard Allen Skinhead books around that time, but this looked like something new and exciting so I handed over my 10p and took it home to read. From that moment on I wanted a motorcycle of my own so I could tear down the streets causing mayhem wherever I went. But it would be another 6 years before that particular dream would come true, when I bought myself a moped. And another year from that before I could legally ride something bigger that the other bikers I hung around with wouldn't laugh at and leave me puttering after them as I desperately tried to keep up.

A love of motorcycles and flying saucers stayed with me for the rest of my life. The bikes have been updated to include electric starts, fairings, fly-screens, heated grips, and all the other luxuries of modern motorcycle life. But for me, flying saucers were always best when they stuck to the original 1950s model. Silvery blue with shooting lasers that incinerate everything they hit. With hostile aliens inside them, not those cute lost traveller types who just want to phone home and fly around on BMX bikes.

This book, like my others, exists because it's a book I wanted to read but couldn't find. But unlike the others, I never set out with the intention of writing it. I needed a trashy B-movie for characters in one of my other books (Meadowside) to go and see at the cinema. I came up with a title, Biker Sluts versus Flying Saucers, a description of the advertising poster, and a couple of action scenes that I wanted the characters to comment on while they watched it. But the more I re-worked those scenes the more I started to realise I wanted to tell Mama Mia's whole story, not just the short snippets I came up with. So I replaced the scenes I had written with scenes from an imaginary film based on one of my other books (Bare Knuckle Bitch), and started making notes for when I would have the time to do it justice as a fully fledged book in its own right.

I knew right from the start it would be set in the 1970s. Modern-day state surveillance and police technology just wouldn't allow Satan's Bastards the sort of free reign they would need in an action/adventure story like the one I wanted to write. And as soon as I decided to set it in 1978, five years after the aliens had wiped out 99% of the Earth's population, I knew it would be more of a biker story than a science fiction one. What 'science' there is, is firmly rooted in 1950s pulp fiction with bug-eyed aliens shooting lasers from flying saucers and wreaking havoc on the world.

And for that I make no apologies whatsoever. So strap on your leather helmet, kick-start your bike, and let's get on with it.

PART 1
THE SHOPPING TRIP

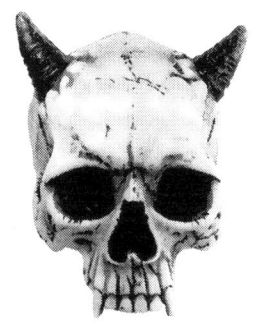

1

Mia always got nervous before a supply run. She'd be daft not to, given the risks involved, but she knew it had to be done. If it was left up to the men they'd eat nothing but swans and rabbits, and sit around smoking dope all day. That was no way for Satan's Bastards to live. They should be out on the road, roaming the country like they used to. Not rotting away in some nature reserve at the arse end of nowhere. So while Mia felt the usual jitters of apprehension, she felt something else too. A tingle of excitement at the prospect of getting back in the saddle and riding away from there. Even if it was only for a few hours.

She picked up the sawn-off shotgun lying beside her sleeping bag and inserted a cartridge in each of the twin barrels. *You can't be too careful out there*, Fat Brenda always drilled into her. That was true, but shotguns were only useful for scaring off packs of wild dogs or as a quick way of getting through locked doors. Against the Angels they were no use at all. Nothing was.

Mia stuffed the loaded shotgun into a backpack and looked around the jumble of possessions littering her tent to see if there was anything else she might need for the shopping trip. A six inch serrated knife and a box of spare shotgun cartridges went into the breast pockets of her leather jacket. She picked up a torch, checked it still worked, and tossed it into the backpack with the shotgun. After another quick look around, she slung the bag over one shoulder and stepped out of the tent into the gathering dusk.

Wicked Tina, Suzy and Margot were waiting for her. Mia looked beyond them to the lake at the far end of the campsite, expecting to see Fat Brenda among the group of men and women watching Bonehead try to light the fire for the night. The winged skull tattoos on each of his biceps bulged as he struck match after match and tossed them at the petrol-soaked damp branches piled up like a skeletal tepee by the side of the lake. He struck another match and threw it at the branches. It extinguished long before it got anywhere near them.

"You need to get a lot closer than that," Tanner said, "and hold it next to the wood when you strike it."

"Yeah right," Bonehead said, "and lose me beard and eyebrows again. Nah, you're all right, I'll do it me own way."

Bonehead struck a match and held it to the remaining matches in the box until they flared up, then tossed the flaming box at the base of the woodpile. The petrol ignited with a whump, and crackling flames shot up the vertical branches. Everyone cheered. Bonehead turned to Tanner and grinned smugly.

"Yeah, well done, Bonehead," Tanner said. He shook his head, but he was smiling at the same time. "Good idea, waste a whole box of matches when one would have been enough."

Bonehead shrugged. "Got the job done, didn't it? Besides, it's shopping day, innit? Just add more matches to the list of shit we need."

Tanner leaned into the flames and lit a huge joint before sitting cross-legged near the fire to smoke it. Bonehead pressed play on his cassette player and a Hawkwind song he had recorded from John Peel's radio show years ago blared out of the tiny speaker.

"Where's FB?" Mia asked, noticing Fat Brenda wasn't part of the group by the fire.

Suzy pointed at one of the tents on the far side of the clearing. "I saw her going in there a while ago."

Mia nodded. "Right. I'll go tell her it's time to go."

Wicked Tina grinned. "Rather you than me, honey."

"Why's that?" Mia asked.

"You'll see," Suzy said.

Mia walked over to the tent Fat Brenda shared with Dirk. Like the other tents, the outside of the green canvas was daubed with white spray-painted slogans — Satan's Bastards, Scum, ACAB, Born to Ride — as well as crooked swastikas and upside-down crosses, anything that would piss off the citizens they had always despised. She opened up the flap and looked inside. Fat Brenda was on her hands and knees on the grass floor, leather trousers around her ankles, while Dirk thrust into her from behind. Rolls of fat rippled with every thrust, like a jelly being smacked with a jack-hammer.

"Christ, FB, you've had all day to do that. Hurry it up, yeah? We're all waiting for you, it's time to go shopping."

Dirk turned his head and grinned at Mia while he continued pounding into Fat Brenda. "Give us another few minutes or so, yeah? Then she's all yours." He slapped Fat Brenda on the arse. She cried out and called him a bastard.

Mia sighed and let the tent flap drop. Wicked Tina, Suzy and Margot, who had followed her over, all burst out laughing.

Mia grinned. "FB might be a while yet, so let's go and wait by the fire for her."

They joined the other bikers by the side of the lake. A few more joints were doing the rounds, and Wicked Tina took a toke on one before she asked what everyone wanted them to look out for. Most wanted booze and smokes, predictably enough. Tanner wanted some new books, said he'd read all the ones they'd got him last time. Basher wanted chicken soup. Skinny Brenda caused a groan from the men and a torrent of insults when she asked for sanitary pads. Even some of the other women joined in with the taunts.

Bonehead held up his joint and offered it to Mia. She raised both hands and shook her head. "Nah, I want to keep a clear head for the ride. Save me some for later though, yeah?"

"I've got a big stash in me tent, we'll share it when you get back," Bonehead said, nodding vigorously.

Mia grinned and nodded back. But Bonehead's eyes were already glazed over, and she knew he would have crashed out long before she returned from the shopping trip.

"Can you get me some more batteries while you're out?" he asked.

Mia smiled. "Yeah, no worries man." Bonehead was always the easiest to please. As long as he had juice for his cassette player and an endless supply of dope to smoke he was as happy as a pig making its first arrest.

"And don't forget the pizza," Basher said with a grin. Everyone laughed.

"Yeah, right," Suzy said, hands on hips. "And I suppose you want bloody ice cream and shit for afters, yeah?"

"Hell, yeah! And some donuts to dip into it!"

"I want bananas and custard," Johnny called out.

"Don't," Wicked Tina said. "Those are one of the few things

I still miss. Why the hell didn't anyone ever think to invent tinned bananas?"

"Wouldn't do you any good if they did," Basher said. "They'd be too mushy to shove up your fanny."

"Piss off, Basher. That was just part of my stage act, and you know it. Besides, the way I remember it, you were the one who ate that banana after I threw it into the audience."

The cannabis-induced giggles came fast and loud. Mia doubted any of them would still be conscious by the time they got back later in the night.

"A rocket launcher would be awesome," someone said.

"Yeah, and a movie projector with something to watch on it."

"That dinosaur one with Raquel Welch in a fur bikini. Gets me hard every time."

"I'll have Raquel Welch, you can shag one of the dinosaurs."

"You guys will get what you get," Fat Brenda said, walking toward the fire with Dirk. Her face was flushed, her cheeks rosy. "If you want anything special you can go out there and get it for yourself."

"Hell no," Dirk said. "That's what you bitches is for. We got much more important shit to do right here." He pulled out a bag of dried magic mushrooms and waved it in the air. Fat Brenda thumped him in the arm and he pretended to be mortally wounded.

Mia smiled. Nobody else would have dared do anything like that to Dirk, and Dirk certainly wouldn't have taken it from anyone but Fat Brenda. Being his old lady obviously came with some privileges, but Mia couldn't help wondering if part of it was down to the sheer intimidating size of the woman. With her tree-trunk arms, huge calloused fists and considerable bodyweight, she could do some serious damage when she wanted to. Mia had seen her flatten seasoned fighters with a single punch on more than one occasion in the old days.

Dirk sat by the fire and opened up the bag of mushrooms. He reached in for a handful and stuffed them into his mouth, then passed the bag on to Tanner in exchange for a toke on his joint. He took a long drag and held his breath, then closed his eyes and exhaled slowly with a sigh. He looked up at Fat Brenda.

"Take care, yeah?" he said. "I'll see you when you get back. And make sure you wear your helmet, just in case you have a spill."

Fat Brenda nodded, then turned away and strode off past the tents and through the bushes on the opposite side of the clearing. Margot bent down and kissed Deano passionately, then followed Fat Brenda. Mia raised a hand to Bonehead. Bonehead, and three other men sitting near him, waved back.

"You ready?" Suzy asked.

Mia nodded. Of course she was ready, she'd been ready for this moment all day. While everyone else slept off their hangovers from the previous night's party, Mia had woken with the dawn chorus. She'd watered Tanner's cannabis crop and gathered wood for the night's fire in a daze, her mind filled with thoughts of the ride to come and the joy it would bring with it.

Her spine tingled as she followed Suzy and Wicked Tina through the bushes and onto the gravel path where the motorcycles were parked. Twenty-eight of them in total, one for each surviving member of Satan's Bastards, all with leather saddle-bags draped over the rear seats from the days when they lived on the road.

Margot and Fat Brenda were sat on their bikes, revving the engines as she approached. Mia walked up to her Norton Commando and mounted it. She lifted a leather helmet and goggles from the front brake lever and put them on, then twisted the key in the ignition. The engine roared into life first time when she stamped down on the kick-start, adding to the noise of the other bikes thrumming beside her.

Fat Brenda pulled forward first on her Triumph Bonneville, closely followed by Margot on her Kawasaki Avenger. Mia watched Suzy and Wicked Tina follow them down the dirt track, their rear wheels throwing up dust as they went, then pulled in the clutch and kicked her bike into gear. She switched on the headlight and rolled forward slowly, both feet scraping along the dirt as she went. She had once dropped her bike on the bend where the dirt track met the main road cutting through the nature reserve after her rear wheel slipped in some mud. That had led to months of taunting about needing stabiliser wheels from the rest of Satan's Bastards, and she was determined it would never happen again.

The others had already sped off into the distance by the time Mia reached the end of the dirt track. She slipped the clutch and dabbed her way onto the tarmac road, then opened up the throttle and accelerated up to thirty. It was a straight road, lined both sides with the silhouettes of tall trees blocking out the stars, and Mia had ridden it so many times over the five years they had been living by the lake she felt she could do it blindfold. She twisted the throttle another inch and whooped in joy as the acceleration tugged at her wrists.

This was what Mia missed the most from the old days. The wind in her face, her long black hair whipping out behind her. The roar of the engine, its heady scent of oil and petrol in her nostrils. The thrill of the ride. It reminded her of those carefree days long ago, when Satan's Bastards were the kings of the road. Riding wherever their bikes took them, doing whatever they wanted, not a care in the world. Travelling from town to town, terrorising the locals, then moving on before law enforcement caught up with them. Another day, another town. Another night, another wild party.

But all that was gone now, and was never coming back.

The Angels had seen to that.

The exit gate came up fast and Mia eased off on the throttle, letting the bike slow itself naturally as she drifted over to the right hand side of the road in preparation. She took the T-junction at twenty, and used the whole width of the main road to accelerate out of the sharp corner. This was another road Mia knew like the back of her hand. She knew every twist and turn, every burnt-out wreck and abandoned vehicle on it. So while the other women rode more cautiously in the cloying darkness, Mia kicked up through the gears and accelerated to sixty.

It didn't take long to catch up with the other bikes. Suzy and Wicked Tina rode two abreast, either side of the dotted white line, trundling along together at a steady fifty, Margot close behind them. Fat Brenda took up the rear, and Mia eased off on the throttle so she could ride alongside her. They cut through woodland, then crossed a river into open farmland. Overgrown fields, long since grown wild, flashed by on both sides, dimly illuminated by the light of the full moon. Wicked Tina and Suzy slowed on the approach to a wrecked Ford Cortina straddling the road, and manoeuvred into single file to navigate around it.

Mia looked up at the sky once she'd passed the car, checking in all directions now her view wasn't obscured by trees and hedgerows. She knew the Angels rarely ventured out at night, but it wasn't unheard of so it always paid to be vigilant. Finding the sky clear, she twisted the throttle and edged ahead of Fat Brenda, then overtook Margot and looked for an opening between Suzy and Wicked Tina. They must have seen her coming because they parted, drifting over to the far left and right sides of the road to make room for her. She waved her thanks as she passed between them, then opened up the throttle wide.

This was what Mia had been waiting for. An open road, and nothing to hold her back, nothing to slow her down. She accelerated up to seventy, a wide grin on her face as the rushing wind took her breath away.

The throaty roar of an accelerating motorcycle came from behind. Mia glanced in her wing mirror and saw Fat Brenda coming up fast. She eased off on the throttle to let the other woman pull alongside in case it was anything important. Fat Brenda grinned at Mia and shouted something, but the words were lost to the roaring wind.

"*What?*" Mia shouted back.

Fat Brenda pulled ahead, waving her left hand as she sped away into the distance. Mia grinned and twisted the throttle another inch, determined not to let her take the lead. If she wanted a race, then she was going to get one, and Mia wasn't going to make it easy for her. Norton versus Triumph, Mia versus Fat Brenda, with the winner getting gloating rights for the rest of the night.

Faster and faster they went down the empty, twisting road. Mia's speedometer nudged eighty. Another twist of the throttle sent it to ninety. Fat Brenda went for the ton and opened up the gap between them. A sharp left-hander came up fast. Mia dabbed her rear brake and drifted over to the centre of the road to get an early view around it. Fat Brenda moved over to the left to take a racing line around the bend, and disappeared from view.

Then she screamed.

Mia instinctively grabbed the front brake and stamped down hard on the rear. She came to a halt at the apex of the bend, just in time to see Fat Brenda fling herself off the back of her bike with her arms splayed. Her motorcycle wobbled down the road under its own steam for another second or so, then crashed down and spun end over end with a shower of sparks before thudding into the underside of a tipped-over lorry straddling the full width of the road.

"FB!" Mia shouted.

Fat Brenda sat up and waved. She struggled to her feet with a grunt and limped toward her wrecked bike, shaking her head and mumbling obscenities to herself. After a few paces she stopped and spun round, then ran full pelt back toward Mia. But before she got very far a deafening explosion knocked her off her feet and sent her sprawling face first in the centre of the road. A huge fireball blossomed out from where her motorcycle had been. Mia ducked down over her petrol tank and covered her face with her hands as the searing shockwave hit her. When she looked up again black clouds of billowing smoke filled her vision.

"FB!" she yelled, kicking down the Norton's side-stand. She jumped off the bike just as the other women pulled up alongside her. Suzy stared open-mouthed at the burning wreckage from astride her Honda 400. Margot jumped off her Kawasaki and ran with Mia, calling out Fat Brenda's name.

"I'm over here," Fat Brenda shouted.

They found her sitting in the road, hands on hips, staring forlornly into the flames. She looked up at Mia and frowned.

"My poor bike."

Mia laughed, relief coursing through her to see Fat Brenda still in one piece. She held out a hand to help her up onto her feet. "You mad cow, you could've killed yourself then, and you're more worried about your stupid bike?"

Fat Brenda shrugged. "I loved that bike."

Mia smiled. "Yeah well, bikes are replaceable, you're not. We'll get you a new one as soon as we can. Same model, same colour, you won't know the difference."

"Or maybe one that's a bit faster?"

Mia laughed and shook her head. "You think that's wise, given what you've just done?"

"Nice firework display," Wicked Tina said, grinning from the seat of her motorcycle when Mia, Fat Brenda and Margot walked out of the smoke together. "I reckoned you was done for, thought I might be in with a chance to take your place in old Dirk's tent."

"Hell no, you skinny bitch," Fat Brenda said, grinning back. "Dirk likes a bit of meat on his woman, he don't go for no titless scrag-ends like you. Besides, it takes more than a little spill like that to put me down for the count." She patted the scuffed leather covering her enormous stomach. "Extra padding comes in useful sometimes."

"Yeah well," Mia said, climbing on her bike. "Looks like we'll need to find another route." She wheeled the bike around to face the way they had come. "And I suppose you'll want a lift?"

Then she glanced up at the sky. Two pulsating blue lights hovered just above the north horizon, growing larger by the second.

"Angels!" she yelled.

2

Mia kicked the Norton into gear and shot forward a split second after Fat Brenda climbed on the back and clutched her around the waist. The extra weight on the back of the bike bottomed out its rear suspension, and Mia felt every bump and pothole she rode over as she sped down the road ahead of Wicked Tina, Suzy and Margot. The lorry behind them still burned bright, illuminating the landscape for miles around. The two flying saucers sped toward it at phenomenal speed.

Mia's heart sank as she watched them grow larger in her wing mirror. She had hoped they would have more time to get away, maybe find somewhere to hole up until it was safe to venture out again. But here they were surrounded by wide open countryside, with the two Angel ships only a few miles away and closing fast. It was only a matter of time before they were spotted, if they hadn't been already. Mia switched off her headlight and accelerated up to fifty, the fastest she dared in the cloying darkness ahead. The other women followed her lead and fell into formation behind her. Mia hoped she wasn't leading them to their deaths.

Another mile down the road, Mia saw the outline of two trees. Just a small oasis of cover, but it was their only chance. As she got closer she saw the trees marked a junction with a B road cutting through the farmland. Mia turned into the junction and came to a halt under the overhang of the trees. The others pulled up alongside her and switched off their engines. Fat Brenda jumped off the back of Mia's bike and pointed at an overgrown wheat field on their left.

"In there, quick!"

Nobody needed telling twice. Mia climbed off her bike and followed the others into the field. She waded through several feet of waist-high yellow stalks, then crouched on the ground and peered through them. The two flying saucers hovered above the burning lorry. Even from a distance, Mia could hear the gentle hum of whatever it was that powered their engines. As she watched, one of the ships broke away and sped off into the distance.

Mia wondered briefly what had caught its attention, and hoped the other would follow it. Instead, the remaining saucer hovered closer to the ground. A cone of harsh blue light shone down from the centre of its underside and illuminated the fields below. Then the ship began sweeping the countryside in slow, zig-zagging straight lines.

"Shit," Fat Brenda said. "We can't stay here, they'll find us straight away. We need to get going."

"And go where?" Margot asked. "We sure as hell can't outrun them."

Mia thought fast. There had to be somewhere nearby they could reach while the Angels were still busy searching the fields on the far side of the lorry. She knew there was nothing for miles back on the main road, so the narrow, twisting B road had to lead somewhere. She just had to hope it led there sooner rather than later.

"Maybe there's a village or something down there," she said, pointing.

"You reckon, honey?" Wicked Tina asked.

Mia shrugged. "I'm just guessing, but this road must go somewhere, otherwise there would be no point having it here."

"Yeah well," Fat Brenda said, standing up, "I hope you're right, but I guess we'll find out soon enough."

They hurried back to their bikes, then set off down the road in single file with their lights switched off. Fat Brenda's immense weight on the back of Mia's bike was even more noticeable at slow speed on the bumpy road, and she wished one of the others had volunteered her a ride instead as she thumped over yet another pothole.

They rode into open countryside, then round a sharp left hand bend and came to a junction with a road sign pointing to a village three quarters of a mile away. They took the turn and soon rumbled into a small farming town, little more than a single row of houses with a small petrol station at its outskirts. They parked the bikes under the petrol station's overhang and Mia just had enough time to plant both feet on the ground before Fat Brenda stood up on the foot-pegs and jumped off.

The petrol station's door and windows had been hastily

boarded up with planks of wood, its owner no doubt worried about looters when they abandoned it. Mia smiled at that thought. As if material goods had mattered at that stage. Maybe the owner thought they would be able to return one day and just carry on as normal once the army had sorted everything out? Like that was ever going to happen. But at least the boards would have kept the wild animals out, and for that Mia was grateful. It meant there might be something inside worth having.

Wicked Tina reached into her left boot and pulled out a dagger with an ivory handle. She jammed it under the edge of one of the boards covering the door and used it like a crowbar to pry the board loose enough to get her fingers under it. Rusted nails groaned and creaked as she pulled the board off, sounding impossibly loud in the silence of the empty village. Mia watched the Angel ship fly over a nearby field, and subconsciously stepped back into the shadows of the building.

Margot and Suzy helped Wicked Tina pull the remaining boards from the door and lay them down in a pile under the boarded up window. Unsurprisingly, the door was locked. Fat Brenda kicked out at it, and it juddered in its frame. Another kick and it slammed back on its hinges. They all crowded around the entrance and peered inside through a cloud of swirling dust. Wicked Tina took out a torch and switched it on.

"Jackpot," Fat Brenda said.

Mia slipped the backpack off her shoulders and took out her own torch. She stepped inside and looked around in awe. The petrol station stocked a wide variety of convenience food, all seemingly untouched since the Angels killed everyone five years ago. Cartons of fruit juice, cans of food, even boxes of breakfast cereal. Four rows of shelves filled with goods, all coated in a thin layer of dust. It had been a long time since she had seen that much food in one place. There was so much of it they would need to make several trips to get it all back to their camp in the nature reserve. But it would certainly be worth it when they returned with a haul like that. They could feast off it for weeks, maybe months.

A faded photograph pinned to a notice board behind the shop's counter caught her eye. It showed a young boy, seven or eight years old, playing with a plastic Angel action figure some enterprising toy company had released soon after their arrival, when everyone still thought they were friendly. Mia couldn't help wondering what had happened to the boy when the killing started. The boards nailed over the door and window indicated his family had been forewarned in some way, but if they had somehow managed to escape then surely they would have returned at some point for the food they left behind?

"Hell yeah," Wicked Tina said excitedly, breaking Mia's train of thought.

She turned to see what had caught her attention. Wicked Tina stood beside a glass-fronted display cabinet filled with bottles. Mia walked over to inspect them for herself. Wicked Tina pulled open the cabinet's door and took out a bottle of whisky. She twisted off the cap and took a long drink, then sighed and wiped her mouth with the back of her hand.

"Now that's what I call a good find," she said, and passed the bottle to Mia. She smiled. "Looks like it's party time, honey."

Mia gulped down a mouthful of whisky, savouring the taste as it burned down her throat and into her stomach, giving her a warm glow inside. She took another long drink before handing the bottle back. Fat Brenda and Suzy headed over for their turn with the bottle, closely followed by Margot.

The remaining bottles in the cabinet began to clink against each other as the Angel ship hovered directly overhead. Thin shafts of blue light surged through gaps between the boards covering the window. Mia held her breath. Everyone else froze, their torches pointed down. They stood in silence for what seemed like forever before the ship moved on, further into the village.

"So what do we bloody well do now?" Suzy whispered.

"We'll have to wait until tomorrow night," Fat Brenda said. "It's not as if we can do anything else, is it? Those bastards will be prowling around out there for hours, and we can't risk going out in daylight, can we?"

Wicked Tina took another hit of whisky and shrugged. "Well I don't know about any of you lot, but I intend to get absolutely wasted," she said. "With all this food and booze we've got here I don't care if we have to stay a month."

Mia frowned. Fat Brenda was right, there was no way they could travel tonight, and venturing out during the day was just asking for trouble. But the idea they might be stuck there for any extended length of time was too depressing to contemplate. She'd rather be back at the camp site, taking up Bonehead's offer of sharing a few joints in his tent.

"Pass me one of them bottles," she said with a sigh.

3

Mia's eyes flickered open. Slivers of harsh sunlight pierced between the boards covering the window, illuminating clouds of swirling dust being kicked up by motorcycle boots clumping around somewhere close by. Outside, birds twittered their dawn chorus, a cacophony of shrill tweets that sent shockwaves of pain through Mia's pounding skull. She groaned and pinched the bridge of her nose, tried to swallow but found her mouth too dry and furry. An empty beer can lay on its side next to her, and the sickly sweet smell coming from its spilled contents made her gag. She lifted her head from the scrunched up leather jacket she'd used as a pillow and pushed herself upright, then arched her back, stretched out her arms, and yawned.

Fat Brenda was chugging on a carton of orange juice, half of it dribbling down her double chin. Mia asked her to pass her one, and she tossed over a fresh carton. Mia blew the dust off it, pulled open the flap, and drained half of it in one gulp before rising groggily to her feet. She yawned again, and rubbed the crown of her head.

"Is there any painkillers? My head's banging."

Fat Brenda shrugged. "Dunno. There probably will be somewhere, they seem to have everything else. But if it's a hangover you've got, more booze is the best cure for that."

Mia's stomach flipped in recoil at Fat Brenda's suggestion. She shuddered, and glanced around the shop. Wicked Tina lay sprawled out on her back, a whisky bottle still clutched in one hand, her wide open mouth emitting a series of regular grunts as she snored away in blissful contentment. Suzy had vomited in her sleep, and the half-digested stale crisps and peanuts she snacked on the night before caked the front of her black leather jacket. Margot lay curled up on her side by the shop counter, surrounded by crushed empty beer cans and a half-full brandy bottle. Mia couldn't help nudging her with her foot as she stepped over her to get at a box of aspirin on a shelf behind the counter. Margot moaned, but didn't wake up.

Mia popped out four of the tablets in the box and washed them down with the remaining orange juice, then dropped the empty carton onto the counter and made her way back through the shop. She picked up her shotgun, walked over to the entrance, and peered out through the gaps between the boards covering the window. It was a bright, sunny day, no clouds in the sky. But more importantly, no sign of any flying saucers or Angels waiting to pounce.

She took a pair of sunglasses from a display rack near the door and put them on, then pulled open the door. It creaked on rusted hinges, causing another moan from Margot. A small animal darted away into the hedgerow opposite, too fast for Mia to tell what it was. She breathed in the cool, early morning air, filling her lungs with its sweet freshness, and stepped outside.

"Where are you going?" Fat Brenda asked.

"To check out the rest of the town."

"What for? There's already more than we can carry right here, so what's the point looking for more stuff?"

Mia shrugged. "You never know, there might be something good. Besides, I said I'd get Tanner some new books, and they haven't got none here."

In reality Mia just wanted a walk in the fresh air to clear her mind and give the aspirin a chance to work its magic on her throbbing head. Listening to Fat Brenda clattering around in her motorcycle boots, along with the snores and moans of the other women, wasn't doing her any good at all.

She headed left into the village and soon came to a newsagents that doubled as the local post office. The door was open, and the sound of scurrying rats came from inside. Mia thought about going inside to see if it had any books, then decided there would be no point. The rats would have chewed them all up by now. She was about to continue when a newspaper hoarding propped up against a wall outside the shop caught her eye. The tattered remains of a five year old Daily Mirror headline read:

ANGELS OR DEMONS?
SHOCK AMERICAN REPORT UNCOVERS THE TRUTH!

Mia sighed and walked on. Too little warning, given far too late. If the world's leaders hadn't been so busy fawning over the Angels in return for photo opportunities they might have recognised them as the threat they turned out to be in time to do something about it. The only consolation, as far as she was concerned, was that those very same world leaders would have been among the first to die when the killing started. She hoped they had all died in agony.

The pavement was cracked and uneven, with tufts of weeds growing between the cracks. The remains of a sheep, little more than bloody tufts of fleece and scraps of bones picked clean by countless scavengers, lay in the road. The houses were all huge compared to the tiny bedsit Mia used to live in before she took up a life on the road with Satan's Bastards. Even with their stained and peeling paintwork, dirty windows and cracked walls overgrown with knotweed, they just oozed affluence. The people who lived in them must have been absolutely loaded, she decided. But now the empty village was just another reminder of what they had all lost. Another ghost town left behind by the Angels, filled with expensive buildings that would one day crumble to nothing.

Satan's Bastards would have had a lot of fun terrorising those people in the old days if they'd come across them. Rich bastards in tiny villages were always easy pickings, and with no cop shop for miles around they could have taken their time with it. Maybe even cut the phone cables and made a weekend of it, like they did once at a similar place they found in Wiltshire. Mia sighed. Those were the best days of her life, and none of it would have ever happened if Satan's Bastards hadn't decided to roll into her home town of Retford all those years ago.

Mia had been waiting tables in The Bouncing Jugs, the town's first and only topless barmaid public house. She was taking an order from a pair of college students while trying to keep out of reach of their groping hands when she heard the roar of dozens of motorcycles pulling up outside.

The door slammed open and everyone turned to stare. Two men walked through together, dressed in filthy jeans and leather jackets. Their hair was long and unkempt, and they both sported long, scraggly beards on their dirty faces. They stood either side of the door like sentries, and glared around the bar while thirty more bikers, both men and women, swarmed inside and made for the far side of the bar, near the jukebox. Middle-aged men already sitting there picked up their drinks and moved away without a word. The bikers eased themselves onto stools and benches, some resting their muddy motorcycle boots on tabletops.

Mia looked at Laura, the head barmaid, to see how she would react to the sudden invasion. Laura stood behind the bar with her arms folded over her bare breasts, glowering at the two men standing by the door. They glowered back. Mia turned her attention to the other bikers. An intricately painted horned skull adorned the back of each of their worn leather jackets, with the phrase SATAN'S BASTARDS printed below it in block capitals.

A morbidly obese woman with long, knotted brown hair rocked the jukebox from side to side. A Dolly Parton song skipped and jumped to its end, to be replaced with Sugar Sugar, a recent novelty song from a TV show Mia couldn't remember the name of. That song got the same treatment, as did the following two singles that fell onto the platter. When the jukebox fell silent, the woman nodded to a bald man with a bushy ginger beard who carried a portable cassette player. He placed the cassette player on top of the jukebox and pressed play. Jimi Hendrix blared out of the speaker, and the fat woman raised her hands above her head and gyrated her enormous hips to the music. Two more women, both stick-thin in comparison, joined her on the impromptu dance floor, while the rest of the bikers whooped and jeered their encouragement.

A hand grabbed Mia's arse. She cried out and spun to face the two students. They laughed. One reached out for her again. She slapped his hand away, a forced smile on her lips. She'd have her pay docked if they complained about the service, and she needed every penny to cover the rent on her bedsit.

"These boys bothering you, miss?" one of the bikers standing by the door asked.

Mia turned toward him, the fake smile still in place. "Nothing I can't handle."

The man nodded, then flashed a grin. There was something odd about him, Mia thought as he walked over to her, and she stared into his dirty face trying to work out what it was. Then she realised. He was looking into her eyes, not staring at her tits like all the other customers did.

"Yeah well," the man said, turning to gaze at the two students, "if that changes, just let me know, yeah?"

The man stood by Mia's side with his arms folded while she took the students' order. He was still there when she returned with two bottled beers and placed them down on the table along with their change. The two students picked their drinks up meekly, avoiding eye contact with Mia as they sipped from them.

"What, you boys don't tip your waitress where you come from?" the man asked. He cracked his knuckles and the two students flinched. They reached into their wallets and pulled out a pound note each, then held them up. The man snatched the money from their hands and gave them to Mia. "Here you go, I reckon you've earned this."

"Thanks," Mia said, pocketing the money.

"I'm Dirk." He gestured at the other biker, who now stood by the bar arguing with Laura. "That there's Deano."

"Mia."

Dirk nodded, then turned away to join Deano at the bar. They both sported the same horned skull design on the back of their leather jackets as the other bikers.

"Is there a problem, miss?" Dirk asked Laura.

"I'm not serving any of you so you might as well go, right now," Laura said.

"What, our money not good enough or something?"

Dirk unzipped a pocket on the side of his leather jacket and pulled out a large wad of cash. He waved it at Laura like a fan, then slammed it down on the bar. Laura's eyes bulged as she stared down at it. She looked up at the two bikers, a frown on her face.

"It's not that," she said, "it's just ... well ..." She looked at Mia, as if she were searching for inspiration, something to say that wouldn't antagonise the two men. "... you know ... I don't think the manager would like it."

Mia shrugged. "I don't see why not, they seem okay to me."

Laura sighed. "Oh what the hell, I only work here. But if anything happens it's on you, Mia, not me. And any damages come out of your pay." She turned back to Dirk. "So what do you want then?"

Dirk tapped a finger on the pile of cash. "Just keep the drinks coming for the rest of the night. If the money runs out before then, come and see me for some more." He gestured at Mia. "Oh, and I want her to serve us, not you. No offence, like, but I don't care much for your attitude."

Dirk turned and wandered away from the bar to join the other bikers, Deano following close behind. Laura scowled at their backs, then picked up the pile of money and counted it, slipping a few five pound notes into her back pocket while she did so.

"Mia," she called out, "go and see what these ... *gentlemen* want to drink. Make a list of everything they order and give it to me, and make sure you don't miss anything out."

The drinks flowed, and the bikers became more and more rowdy as the night progressed. Laura remained behind the bar, watching on while Mia supplied them with fresh bottles of beer and took away the empties. One by one the regular customers left, and the bikers spread out through the bar to take up the vacated seats. The Rolling Stones blasted out of the cassette player, which Dirk had turned up to maximum volume, and they all shouted to one another over the distorted music.

They seemed friendly enough to Mia, despite their rough outward appearance, and seemed genuinely interested in her life outside work. The overweight woman even offered Mia her leather jacket to cover herself up with. Mia took it gratefully and shuffled into it, ignoring Laura's scowl of disapproval from the bar. They were supposed to remain topless at all times during opening hours, but with nobody around to ogle her Mia didn't see the point. The jacket was huge, and Mia could have easily wrapped it around herself twice over. Instead she just zipped it up and let it hang from her shoulders like a giant leather poncho.

"I'm Fat Brenda," the woman said.

Mia smiled and shook her head. "I can't call you that."

Fat Brenda shrugged. "Why not? It's my name, and it'll save a lot of confusion with Skinny Brenda over there." She pointed across the table at one of the other women sitting with her. Skinny Brenda smiled and raised a hand in greeting.

"I think I'll call you Brenda One and Brenda Two, if that's all right with you?"

Fat Brenda shrugged again. "Yeah, whatever."

"How come she gets to be Brenda One?" Skinny Brenda asked.

"We could take turns, if you want? You can be Brenda One for the next hour, I'll be Brenda One for the hour after that. How's that sound?"

Mia laughed and raised her hands. "Yeah, okay, you win." She pointed at Fat Brenda. "You, I'll call FB. And you," she added, pointing at Skinny Brenda, "I'll call SB. How's that?"

Skinny Brenda raised a thumb and smiled. Fat Brenda grunted.

"Randy Mandy," one of the other women said.

"I'm Wicked Tina, honey."

"Juicy Lucy."

"I'm just plain old Suzy," another said.

Mia nodded to each of them in turn, recognising Suzy and Wicked Tina as the ones who had danced with Fat Brenda earlier in the night.

"So how come they call you Wicked Tina then?"

"It was my stage name back when I was stripping, and it kind of stuck. That's how I first met these guys, they came to one of my shows. A right rowdy bunch they were, too." She laughed. "They kept trying to pinch my whip."

Mia asked about the biker lifestyle, where they were from, and what they did. She was surprised to find out the women all had their own motorcycles, they weren't just girlfriends tagging along with the men like she had assumed. She learned Fat Brenda was Dirk's 'old lady' which, seemed to mean they were a steady couple. Margot, a short woman with long black hair sitting at the opposite end of the bar, was Deano's old lady. The others were 'mamas' — free spirits who belonged to nobody and would hook up with any man they felt like whenever the mood took them, with no strings attached.

None of the bikers were from any particular town or geographical area, they had just drifted together over the years on the road, or met up at music festivals and decided to travel together. The horned skull, and the name Satan's Bastards below it, bonded them together stronger than any family ever could. They would die for each other if they had to, and if one of them was in trouble they would sort it out together, no matter what it took.

Mia found the women easy to talk to, and opened up to

them about her own life, all the shitty dead-end jobs she had worked since leaving school two years earlier. About the foster home she grew up in after her parents dumped her, how the home's owners cared more about the cash handouts they got from the government than they did about the seventeen young children in their charge. The women listened, nodding sympathetically while it all poured out of her. The tiny bedsit that swallowed up almost half her wages. Her supervisor, Laura, who undermined her at every opportunity. Her boss, Mike Silvers, the fat, balding owner of The Bouncing Jugs and his wandering hands at closing time.

"You ever thought of giving it all up?" Fat Brenda asked.

"And do what? Go on the dole? No thanks."

"There's more than one way to earn a living, honey," Wicked Tina said.

Fat Brenda laughed. "Speaking of which, what time do you get off work, Mia?"

"About half-ten, after the boss gets here to cash up. That's if the dirty old bastard doesn't want me to stay behind for what he calls extra duties."

"Well if I were you, I'd get myself home straight away, as soon as you can."

"Why?"

"You're a good person, Mia," Fat Brenda said with a shrug. "Most citizens wouldn't give scum like us the time of day. Listen, you like to party, right?"

"Yeah, sure, who doesn't?"

"We're camped out in the woods by the canal, we'll be there another couple of days or so, why don't you come along and see us before we move on? I'll take you for a ride on my bike, show you what you're missing."

A low growl snapped Mia back to the present. A rake-thin dog stood half in, half out of the hedgerow on the opposite side of the road. Crouched down on its haunches, it pulled back its lips to reveal a mouth full of sharp, blood-stained teeth. Its ears were almost flat against its head, its eyes wide, its tail upright and quivering. It stared straight at Mia and snarled as it crept forward like a cat stalking its prey.

4

Mia cursed herself as she raised the shotgun and aimed at the dog. She'd been stupid to let her mind wander like that. She was lucky it was just a dog, and not an Angel patrol she'd wandered into.

"Go on, get out of it," she yelled.

But the dog continued its slow approach, its teeth bared.

Then seven more dogs appeared from the hedgerow behind it, all just as malnourished as the first.

Mia's finger curled around the trigger of her shotgun, but she knew she wouldn't be able to shoot them all. She only had the two cartridges in the gun, and even if she hadn't left the rest of them in her leather jacket back at the petrol station there wouldn't be enough time to reload before the dogs pounced.

"Nice doggies," she said quietly as she backed away. "Stay."

One of the older dogs, a golden Labrador with half an ear missing, wagged its tail a couple of times. Another dog, this one much younger, growled and snapped at it, and the Labrador's tail drooped between its legs.

Mia backed into a wooden fence surrounding one of the houses. She startled and glanced over her shoulder, then edged her way along the fence until she came to a closed gate. Keeping her eyes on the approaching dogs, she reached behind her for the latch and nudged the gate open with the heel of her boot. She darted through the gate and slammed it behind her, then ran through the front garden. The leading dog jumped over the fence, barking furiously, closely followed by two more.

Mia ran for a metal dustbin at the side of the house and bounded onto it, reaching out for a drainpipe to keep her balance. A dog jumped up at her and clamped its jaws around the heel of her motorcycle boot. Mia spun and kicked it in the side of the head with her other boot. The dog yelped and fell away, then jumped up again with a snarl. The remaining dogs barked as they ran through the front garden to join it.

Mia stuffed the shotgun's barrel down the front of her jeans and grabbed the drainpipe in both hands, then hefted herself up, her feet scrabbling for purchase against the wall. She looked up and saw a small window above, three feet to the left of the drainpipe, and climbed up toward it. One of the dogs jumped onto the dustbin and stretched up with its front paws against the wall. It snapped at Mia's heels, then barked, as if it were demanding she come back down so it could eat her.

Mia's foot slipped and she cried out as her body swung to one side and slammed into the wall. Before she could do anything to stop it, the shotgun flew out of her jeans and clattered to the ground. One of the dogs pounced on it and bit the wooden stock. Mia found her footing again, then continued climbing up the drainpipe until she was adjacent to the window. She swung out her left leg and kicked at the window pane with the toe of her boot. The glass held strong, the rotting wooden frame more sturdy than it looked.

Mia gained a footing on the window ledge, then reached out for the trim at its side. She rested a couple of seconds with her arms and legs splayed, her breath coming in short pants, then with a cry of determination she let go of the drainpipe and hauled herself across the short gap, shuffling her feet along the narrow ledge until she could grab the trim at both sides of the window to hold herself in place. She glanced down at where the shotgun had fallen. The pack of dogs stared up at her. One licked its lips.

Mia raised a knee and kicked out at the window with the sole of her boot. It took two more attempts before the glass shattered inward with a loud crash. The stench hit her immediately. Putrid, cloying, like rotten meat left out in the sun. She gagged, and swallowed the resulting mouthful of orange-tasting bile back down. The dogs were barking again, and jumping up at the wall. They must have known their prey had found an escape route they wouldn't be able to follow.

Mia kicked out jagged shards of glass from the edges of the window frame, then swung herself into the house. She found herself in a landing, stairs to her right, a bathroom to her left. Two bedroom doors, both wide open, stood a short distance away. The rotten stench drifted out from both bedrooms, and she could taste it in her throat. She gagged again and ran into the bathroom, leaned over the sink and vomited. She turned on both taps to rinse it away. Nothing came out of the cold tap, but brown, stagnant water came from the other.

Mia cupped her hands and splashed dirty water over her face. She thought about using some of it to rinse the foul acidic taste from her mouth, then thought better of it. The water would have been stood in the immersion tank for over five years, and there was no telling what kind of bacteria could have grown in it during that time. She spat into the sink and checked the cabinet mounted above it.

It contained three toothbrushes, a tube of toothpaste squeezed in the middle, a bottle of mouthwash, a battery operated shaver, a jar of Vicks Vaporub, cotton buds, cough mixture, a box of aspirin, and a hairbrush with strands of long blonde hair attached to it.

Mia opened the bottle of mouthwash and took a swig, swilled it around her mouth and spat in the sink. She pocketed the aspirin and cough mixture and was about to leave the bathroom when she stopped and turned back to look at the Vaporub. She twisted off the lid and sniffed it, then applied a thick blob to her top lip to counteract the smell drifting out of the bedrooms and made her way downstairs.

The hallway was surprisingly spacious, much bigger than the shared entrance to Mia's bedsit, with a closet built into the space beneath the stairs. She looked inside and saw coats and scarves hanging from rails, beneath them a jumble of toys in a wooden box, several pairs of shoes, and a plastic bucket containing wash leathers for cleaning windows. A blue rotary dial telephone stood on a table near the front door, with a notepad and pen lying next to it. Family photographs hung on the wall in a neat row, showing a smiling couple and a young girl in various exotic foreign locations.

Mia hated the child instantly. Resented the fact that it had such loving parents, while hers had just thrown her away like so much unwanted trash. She wondered if her own parents had lived in a posh house like this. Wondered if they had gone on to have another child, one they had actually kept and looked after instead of discarding it like they had with her.

A dog jumped up at the front door with a snarl. The door handle rattled. Mia ran to the door and checked it was locked, then drew deadbolts top and bottom to make extra sure the dogs couldn't get in. She leaned back against it and looked around while she considered her options. Three doors, one open, the others closed. The door closest to her had a small bathroom-type bolt set high up in its frame. Mia reached up and unlocked it, then pushed the door open.

A huge grand piano took pride of place in the centre of the room, the walls around it covered with dozens of horizontal swords resting on wooden hooks. Mia walked over to the front window and peered out. Two of the dogs stood in the garden, staring at the front door while another stood upright on its hind legs, its jaws clamped around the handle as if it were trying to jerk it open.

One of the dogs must have sensed Mia's gaze, because its head snapped round to stare at her. It bared its teeth and growled. The other dogs ran up to the window, barking furiously, and jumped up at it. Mia drew the curtains, hoping they would go away if they couldn't see her, and turned away to inspect the swords on the wall. She pulled one down and felt its edge. It was blunt, nothing but a decoration. Even its tip had been rounded so it couldn't injure anyone.

"Shit."

She put the sword back on its hooks and checked the other rooms. One was a kitchen filled with the latest appliances, dusty grain-effect Formica covering every surface. She headed for a large white fridge taller than herself and pulled open the door. It smelled of rotting eggs, and the shelves were filled with the furry remains of what could have been anything.

Mia found what she was looking for on a shelf at the bottom of the fridge door, a can of cola. She grabbed it and tore it open, tossing the ring-pull onto the kitchen floor. She gulped the warm, sugary drink down and sighed, then walked up to the kitchen window and looked out. Another dog stood in the back garden, facing the house. Mia stepped back into the shadows before it noticed her. How the hell were they intelligent enough to surround the house like that? They were just dogs, not people.

A huge, 24 inch colour television took pride of place in the spacious living room, built into a solid wooden cabinet with intricate carving on each of its four legs. It was the biggest television Mia had ever seen, and she couldn't even guess at how much it would have cost. Probably more than she used to make in a whole year when she worked at The Bouncing Jugs. Plush leather armchairs and a three-seater settee covered in pink cushions were positioned around the television. A silver music centre stood atop a glass-fronted cabinet filled with expensive-looking brass ornaments. A book case took up an entire wall, its shelves crammed with leather volumes.

Mia went over to the book case and studied the titles, but saw nothing Tanner would be interested in reading. Most of them were encyclopaedias and history books, filled with useless facts that didn't matter any more. The only fiction she saw were the books she had been forced to read at school — Charles Dickens, Thomas Hardy, Harper Lee, Jane Austen, Shakespeare, crap like that. All the books that had been so boring they had put her off reading for life, so why anyone would want to own those books was beyond her. Tanner liked books about Hells Angels and skinheads, monsters and serial killers. Those were the books they should have studied at school, books people actually wanted to read.

The last book Mia had tried to read was A Clockwork Orange, after going to see the movie with the rest of Satan's Bastards three years before the Angels first arrived. She had loved that film so much she couldn't resist taking a peek at Tanner's paperback version after he proclaimed it the best book he had ever read. Mia didn't see the attraction, and gave up after a few pages. It was written in some sort of gobbledegook language, and she spent so much time looking at the dictionary printed at the back of the book to decipher it she couldn't follow the story.

Mia looked out of the window. The dog still prowled the back garden like a lion circling an injured zebra. Mia sat down in one of the leather armchairs and finished off the can of cola, then crushed the can and tossed it into the fireplace. What the hell was she supposed to do now? If she opened any of the doors they would hear her and come running.

She thought about getting a sharp knife from the kitchen to replace the one she had left back at the petrol station to defend herself with, but if they all attacked at once she would have no chance against them. Maybe they would just get bored and go away? But that could take hours, and even then they would probably lie in wait for her in the hedgerow opposite the house, ready to pounce out when she was least expecting it. What she needed to do was get them all in the back garden, then keep them occupied long enough for her to sneak out of the front door.

Some food, that would do it. The dogs all looked emaciated, so they would certainly go straight for any food tossed out of an upstairs window. Maybe she could find something to poison it with first? No, then they might be able to smell the poison, and wouldn't go for the food. Or it might take so long to work she'd be stuck there for days.

Mia stood up and went back into the kitchen, picking up the plastic bucket from the closet under the stairs on the way. She searched the larder, but there was very little food in it. Just two small cans of dog food, a packet of dried rice, and half a packet of Smash instant mash that had got damp and had mould growing on it. Mia emptied them all into the bucket and stirred the concoction with a wooden spoon she found in a drawer under the sink, then added some water from a kettle on the stove to bulk it out and carried it upstairs.

The putrid smell still permeated her nostrils, even over the Vicks Vaporub she had hoped would mask it. She lifted the neck of her T-shirt and held it over her nose and mouth as she stepped into the back bedroom. Posters of Donny Osmond and David Cassidy smiled down at her from the far wall. A large dolls' house stood in one corner, the front of the house opened up to reveal rooms inside crammed full of miniature furniture and tiny jointed figures. Next to the dolls' house was a single bed surrounded by teddy bears and stuffed toy animals.

In the bed, cuddled up to a large golliwog with one eye missing, lay the mummified remains of a young girl, no more than eight years of age, with long blonde hair lovingly platted into two pigtails. Her skin was withered and grey, stretched tight around her face to pull her mouth into a permanent rictus grin revealing perfectly straight but yellowed teeth. Her eyes had long since shrivelled away, the eyelids covering them sunk deep into the sockets.

Mia drew back the curtains and opened the window. The

dog in the back garden looked up and barked as she leaned out.

"Hey dog," she shouted, "I've got something for you."

Another dog bounded into the garden from the side of the house. Mia slapped the palm of her hand against the outside of the window a couple of times.

"Dinner time, come and get it!"

She waited until two more dogs came to investigate, then poured a small amount of slop from the bucket. It splattered onto the concrete below and the dogs ran for it. They snarled and snapped at each other as they fought over the food, gulping it down as fast as they could. When it was all gone they looked up at Mia and licked their lips. The Labrador wagged its tail. Three more dogs wandered into the back garden, their noses twitching. Mia counted them, seven in total. One dog still unaccounted for.

"Din-dins," she shouted in a cheerful, sing-song voice. "Missing doggie, where are you?"

The remaining dog darted into the back garden and joined the others standing under the bedroom window. Mia swung the bucket and hurled it as far into the garden as she could, then ran back downstairs. She slid open the two bolts on the front door, twisted the latch, and swung the door open. She listened to the dogs fighting over the food in the back garden to make sure they were still occupied, then crept around the side of the house to pick up the shotgun and ran through the gate, out onto the street, and back down it.

5

The other women were all up and about when Mia got back to the petrol station. Wicked Tina sat side-saddle on her bike, chugging from a bottle of beer. She raised a hand and waved when she saw Mia approach. Suzy and Margot were loading canned foods into the saddle-bags attached to the rear of their motorcycles. Suzy looked up as she fastened a strap on one of the bags.

"Where've you been then?" she asked.

Mia shrugged. "Just went for a walk, that's all. Listen, there's a pack of dogs just down the road so we need to watch out for them. Where's FB?"

"In the shop," Suzy said.

"I'll go and let her know," Mia said as she walked over to the doorway.

Fat Brenda had her arms full of cartons of cigarettes. An over-stuffed backpack rattled and clinked with tin cans and bottles while she tried to cram them inside it. Mia told her about the dogs, how they had trapped her in the house and surrounded it. How they seemed to know how to open doors, and how she had finally managed to escape from them.

"Good thinking," Fat Brenda said.

"So what's the plan?" Mia asked. "Are we going now, or waiting until tonight?"

"Dunno, let me check outside first."

Fat Brenda carried the backpack outside and leaned it against the rear wheel of Mia's Norton Commando. Mia followed her out and noticed her saddle-bags were also overflowing with goods, and hoped someone had remembered Bonehead's batteries. She decided she'd slip a few packs into her leather jacket later, just in case. That just left Tanner's books, but there was nothing she could do about that and she certainly wasn't going to risk breaking into any of the other houses to look for some with those dogs prowling around.

Fat Brenda cupped a hand over her eyes and gazed up at the cloudless sky in all directions. "Well there's no sign of any Angels yet, but I don't know how long that will last. Probably best to wait until night, just in case. We don't want to get caught out in the open again, it's too risky."

"Nah," Margot said. "They'll be long gone by now, so I say we might as well get going now. If we keep a look out for them we should be okay, it's not like we've got far to go."

"There's more of them around in the day though," Fat Brenda said, "and they're harder to see without their lights."

Margot shrugged. "Yeah well, so are we."

"I reckon we should stay a few more days, just to make sure," Wicked Tina called out from her bike.

Mia smiled. "Nah, you just don't want to leave all that booze behind."

"Yeah, well? I didn't see you turn any down last night, honey."

"That was last night, we didn't have no choice then," Mia said. "Besides, now we know about this stash we can always come back to it later, maybe fetch a few of the guys next time to help us carry it all. I say we wait until night. There's no point taking risks when we don't need to."

Wicked Tina frowned, then shrugged and lifted the beer bottle to her lips. She drained it and tossed it away into the hedgerow. "Yeah well," she said, "as long as we board it all up again so them dogs of yours can't get in. I might need to make a few midnight trips by myself over the next few days, and I don't want no surprises when I do."

The decision was made, they would leave at nightfall. They spent the rest of the day packing as much as they could carry, and ate their fill from what they were leaving behind. At dusk, Mia tossed the empty food cans into the hedgerow so the dogs wouldn't be able to smell them anywhere near the petrol station, while Suzy helped Wicked Tina board up the door again, using one of her motorcycle boots for a hammer. When they were ready to go, Mia climbed on her bike and retrieved her helmet and goggles from the front brake lever, then nodded at Fat Brenda to get on the back.

The others kick-started their bikes and pulled forward. Mia wobbled after them, her suspension bottomed out by saddle-bags crammed full of canned food and Fat Brenda's overflowing backpack adding to her own immense bulk. But once she got up to speed back on the main road she soon forgot about the excess weight and let the thrill of the ride take over. She couldn't wait to show Bonehead all the great stuff they'd found, and tell him about all the extra booze they'd had to leave behind. Maybe he'd fancy a trip back there with her later in the night after everyone was asleep, so they could have their own little private party.

Back at the nature reserve, Mia caught the scent of burnt meat cooking over an open fire as she rode down the tarmac road, and wondered what sort of animal the men had hunted that day. She didn't recognise the smell, but that was no surprise. With pickings from the supply runs becoming more and more scarce none of them cared much anymore what they ate. If it had four legs and a tail it was fair game. Even the geese from the island in the middle of the lake ended up on a spit if they weren't quick enough to get out of the way in time. But Mia was certain they would throw whatever it was they were cooking away as soon as they caught sight of all the goodies their latest haul contained.

Margot turned off onto the dirt track. Mia brought her bike to a halt and put down her feet.

"You'll have to walk the rest of the way," she said over her shoulder to Fat Brenda.

"How come?"

"I'm still not too confident on dirt tracks, I like something solid under my wheels."

Fat Brenda sighed. Mia gripped the handlebars tight and braced herself while Fat Brenda grabbed her shoulders and stood up on the rear foot-pegs. Suzy dabbed her way past Mia's bike, onto the dirt track, and rode away with a wave. Wicked Tina pulled up behind and waited while Fat Brenda hopped off Mia's bike.

"Well I'll see you there then," Fat Brenda said curtly as she set off walking down the dirt track with her backpack clanking.

Mia frowned. It was obvious from the woman's tone of voice she wasn't happy about the enforced exercise. She glanced over her shoulder and shrugged at Wicked Tina, then dabbed her bike forward to make room for her to turn onto the dirt track. After she had gone, Mia rolled her bike back, turning the handlebars to line it up to take the turn head-on, then set off slowly with her feet scraping the dirt. When she caught up with Fat Brenda's plodding pace she slowed to a crawl and slipped the clutch to walk the bike behind her.

Fat Brenda wouldn't look at her, and refused to acknowledge any of Mia's attempts at conversation, so she gave up and followed her the rest of the way in silence. At the end of the track Mia parked her bike alongside the others and climbed off to walk the short distance to the campsite by the lake. It seemed odd Skinny Brenda and Randy Mandy hadn't come to help them unpack like they usually did. They must have heard the bikes arrive because it was pretty quiet. Mia couldn't even hear Bonehead's cassette player, which seemed odd. Maybe its batteries had run out or something.

"You won't be needing any of that rancid meat," Mia called out as she approached the bushes surrounding the campsite, "not when you see all the stuff we've ..."

Her voice trailed off when Fat Brenda gave out a roar of anguish. With a feeling of dread she darted through the bushes to see what had caused it.

Charred, smoking bodies lay everywhere she looked. Yellow fat dripped from blistered, peeling skin. Thick, grey fluid oozed from empty eye sockets and dribbled down exposed cheekbones. Yellow teeth grinned out from blackened, hairless faces with no lips or cheeks. Scorched motorcycle boots and leather jackets clung to some of the bodies, the only clothing not incinerated.

More bodies floated face down in the lake, just as burnt as the ones on land. A crow stood on the back of one of them, its beak buried deep in the cooked flesh of the corpse's exposed and blackened buttocks. It ripped off a shard of meat and swallowed it, then went back for more. Fat Brenda ran over and splashed into the water, chased the bird away, then fell to her knees and sobbed into her hands. Wicked Tina looked up at the sky and screamed abuse at it, her fists clenched. Suzy and Margot stood stock still and stared at the devastation before them, their eyes wide, their mouths hanging open.

Mia bent over and a fountain of vomit spewed from her mouth. She continued retching long after her stomach emptied.

6

Tears streamed down Mia's cheeks as she stared down at the huge shallow grave filled with the burnt remains of the only real family she had ever known. The only people who had ever looked out for her, the only ones who had ever really cared. The rag-tag army of men and women who had taken her under their wing and made her truly happy for the first time in her entire life.

Deano and Tanner, who both offered to break her boss's fingers when she told them she had been sacked from her job at The Bouncing Jugs after Laura had blamed her for what happened that night. Skinny Brenda, who gave her a ride on the back of her BSA Bantam and a place in her tent when Satan's Bastards moved on from Retford and she asked if she could go with them.

Skitter, who taught her how to ride his motorcycle and never once complained at all the indicators and mirrors he had to replace every time she dropped it, or the extra dents and scratches she added to its petrol tank and side panels when she crashed it. All the other men and women, who had clubbed together to buy her a motorcycle of her own once she got the hang of it. And Randy Mandy, who had painted the horned skull insignia on the back of a leather jacket in secret and presented it to her along with the bike.

But most of all Bonehead, who had always been there for her whenever she needed him. He'd never gone as far as making her his old lady, but Mia knew she was his favourite lover, just as much as he was hers. They had been almost exclusive to each other for over a year, so it would have only been a matter of time before they made it official.

But now he was gone, snuffed out along with the rest of Satan's Bastards like so much trash. She couldn't even tell which one he was, that was the worst part. All the tattoos he was so proud of had been burnt away with the rest of his flesh.

She'd never see those winged skulls on his biceps again, or the grim reaper riding a motorcycle across his chest. Never feel his touch. Never smell his musky scent as he made love to her. Because it *was* love, she was sure of that. He'd never say it, of course, that wasn't his way. But she knew deep down he felt the same way she did about him. Now he just lay there somewhere before her, in an unmarked grave where the tents used to stand. Surrounded by his family.

Mia choked back a sob. She felt empty inside. Like her heart had been ripped out of her. None of the other women standing around the mass grave spoke. There was nothing to say. Nothing they could do but stare down at the charred bodies, lost in their own thoughts.

Fat Brenda had retrieved the keys from the motorcycles of each of them while Mia, Suzy, Margot and Wicked Tina dug the grave. She'd bawled her eyes out while they dragged the bodies into it and lay them side by side. But her tears had long since dried up, her misery replaced with stoic defiance as she climbed down into the grave and placed a single key on the chest of each corpse lying there.

Mia knew it was an empty gesture. Other than Tanner, who still wore his brass bullet belt, there was no way of matching the right key to the right body. So she didn't comment on it when she saw Fat Brenda palm one of the keys and slip it into her pocket before she climbed back out. The woman would need a bike of her own now she had wrecked hers, and whoever the one she had chosen used to belong to wouldn't begrudge her that.

Suzy and Wicked Tina used their shovels to toss loose earth over the bodies. Mia picked up another shovel and joined them, while Margot and Fat Brenda stood by and watched. When the grave was filled in, Fat Brenda turned and walked away. Mia assumed she wanted to be alone, and joined the others to sit cross-legged around the grave in silence. She thought about all the good friends she had lost, and tried hard to think only of the good times they had spent together. But her mind kept wandering back to the night the Angels first arrived on earth. The night that everything changed forever.

Funds were running low after a summer filled with music festivals and drugs, travelling up and down the country to meet up with old acquaintances and allies, as well as settle some old scores with past enemies. All Satan's Bastards had left was the emergency cash held in reserve for bribing police officers with when they were stopped at the roadside, so it was time to replenish the coffers to see them through the autumn and winter months.

As soon as Mia walked through the door of The Crippled Stag in Gainsborough that night she knew Dirk had made the right choice. The place was heaving with young, long-haired men and women in flared trousers, the drinks flowing fast, the tills filling up with banknotes ripe for the taking. While a few customers turned to gawp at them when the bikers swarmed inside, most just ignored them and continued with their loud conversations.

David Bowie's Starman blasted out of the jukebox, accompanied by raucous, drunken singing from a group of Bowie wannabes swaying before it in their Ziggy Stardust makeup and white satin shirts. Two young women in miniskirts played pool nearby, generating a loud cheer from the male onlookers each time they bent over the table to take a shot.

Match of the Day playing on a black and white television mounted high up on a shelf at the opposite side of the bar competed with the jukebox for volume, the sounds mingling together in the centre into one cacophonous noise. A large group of men in football shirts crowded around the television and shouted encouragement when the striker took a shot, then groaned as one when the goalkeeper caught the ball and kicked it away.

The bikers elbowed their way through the crowd hovering around the bar. The bar staff, two men and a woman, all in their mid-twenties and wearing jeans and T-shirts, looked at them expectantly, with no trace of fear or nervousness at their massed ranks. Mia liked that, and couldn't help feeling a pang of regret about the way she knew the night would end for them. In the four years she had been with Satan's Bastards Mia had found such acceptance among citizens very rare. Most outsiders they came into contact with showed nothing but open contempt, and got what they deserved when they were left bloodied and battered. But with these three, Mia hoped they wouldn't put up too much of a fight when the time came. That they would accept what was happening with grace and save themselves a beating.

Dirk pulled out the emergency wad of cash and waved it in the air. The barmaid smiled and made her way straight for him.

"Whatever they all want to drink," Dirk shouted over the blaring music. "And get one for yourself and your two mates over there while you're at it."

The barmaid raised a thumb and nodded, then went over to her colleagues to pass the order on. The bikers all shouted at once, and the bar staff hurried to serve them. Most wanted whisky chasers with their beer, to compensate for their late arrival and make up for lost time, but Mia settled on just a bottled lager. She wanted to keep her wits about her until the job was done, and she knew from past experience there would be plenty of time to get blind stinking drunk later, once it was all over and they had the place to themselves.

When everyone had their drinks they turned and made their way to the jukebox side of the bar. Bonehead squeezed himself onto the end of a padded bench and put his cassette player down on the table. The group of young David Bowie lookalikes already sitting there shuffled closer together to make room for him. One sniffed and wrinkled his nose at the stench wafting from the filthy sleeveless denim jacket Bonehead wore over his leathers. Bonehead glared across the table at more youths sitting on stools opposite while he took a long drink, then slammed the glass down on the table and cracked his knuckles.

"You boys going to be here much longer?" he asked. "Only my brothers and sisters here don't like to stand up for too long."

The youths on the stools spun around and gaped at the bikers staring down at them. A couple stood up and wandered away, muttering to each other. Stevo and Basher took up their seats. Basher took out a knife and pressed a switch on the side of its handle. A six inch blade shot out. Basher splayed his left hand on the table's surface, then began stabbing the wood between each of his fingers while he stared across at the David Bowies sitting on the bench. Three more peeled away and Dirk, Fat Brenda and Randy Mandy squeezed into the space they left behind. Another Bowie stood to leave and looked down at Bonehead, who was blocking his exit.

"Um ... excuse me," he said.

Bonehead looked up with a sneer. "Yeah?"

"Um ... I need the toilet?"

"Do I look like your mother or something?" Bonehead picked up his beer and took another swig. "If you need someone to hold it for you, just ask the ladies. I'm sure one of them will oblige."

"No, I mean I need to get past."

"So what's stopping you?"

"Well, um ..."

Bonehead's hand shot up. Bowie flinched. Bonehead leaned back in his seat and scratched the back of his bald head. He sighed, then shuffled himself upright and swung his feet under the bench. He stroked his long, scraggly ginger beard and pulled a small twig from it, looked at it in confusion for a second, then flicked it at Basher.

"Thanks," Bowie said as he squeezed past.

But before he could get far, Bonehead's hand shot out and grabbed him by the arm.

"You got a light?" he asked.

"Um, yeah, sure." The Bowie clone's hand shook as he took out a box of Swan Vestas and handed it to Bonehead.

"Cheers. You got a cigarette to go with it?"

"Um ... yeah, no problem." He reached into his pocket for a pack of Lambert and Butler, then pulled out a cigarette and held it out. Bonehead snatched the whole pack from the man's hand instead.

"Cheers mate, I really appreciate it."

Bowie stared at Bonehead, wide-eyed. He bit his lip and looked like he was about to say something, then changed his mind and walked away shaking his head. Mia straddled Bonehead's lap and kissed the top of his bald head as she climbed over him onto the bench. Bonehead tossed her a cigarette and lit one for himself before holding out the flaming match to her. As Mia leaned in and puffed on her cigarette, a loud groan came from the crowd watching the football. Presumably another missed goal opportunity.

The remaining two Bowies sandwiched between Mia and Dirk looked at each other nervously, then crawled under the table to make their escape. Tanner and Margot took their place by climbing over Dirk, Fat Brenda and Randy Mandy, stepping between them on the padded bench.

Someone unplugged the jukebox, and Gary Glitter slowed to a warbling halt mid-song. The volume on the television at the other end of the bar increased, and one by one everyone fell silent as they caught part of the news flash that had interrupted the football.

"... which appear to be some form of flying saucers of unknown origin," a newsreader said. "It is not known at this stage if there is any hostile intent, therefore the public are urged to keep away for their own safety."

"What did he say?" Mia asked. She leaned forward and craned her neck to stare at the television as the newsreader continued. It had to be some sort of joke. Flying saucers weren't real, everyone knew that.

The flickering screen showed a shaky image of dozens of aircraft of a type she had never seen before, obviously filmed with a hand-held telephoto lens from a long distance away. They were a flat circular shape with a round ball in the centre, dull grey in colour, and were clustered in what looked like an overgrown field in the middle of nowhere.

"Unconfirmed reports are coming in of identical flying saucers being seen in other remote parts of the world. We will bring you more on that as the news comes in, but for now we have leading astronomer Patrick Moore on the line for his comments. Patrick, why wasn't the existence of these alien spacecraft picked up when they entered our solar system?"

"Well Peter, first of all there is no evidence these craft are indeed of alien origin. And secondly if they are, which logic would dictate is extremely unlikely, as you may know the Mark I Lovell radio telescope at Jodrell Bank suffered a minor fault in the storms several days ago which rendered it inoperable until earlier this evening."

"What about NASA? Surely Skylab would have picked them up, so why are we only now hearing about their existence?"

"Skylab has many functions, but long range space observation is not one of them, so even if they were, and I stress the word if, of extraterrestrial origin Skylab would not have given us any warning of their existence. What we are seeing here is much more likely to be ..."

Mia glanced at Bonehead while the interview continued. "You think it's true?"

Bonehead shrugged. "Don't know, don't care. It doesn't

affect me either way."

"Yeah but come on, *flying saucers*? Aren't you even a little bit curious about what's inside them, or why they are here?"

"Why would I be?"

Mia shook her head and turned her attention back to the television. Trust Bonehead to be unimpressed by something as monumental as this. Of course it would affect him. It changed everything. They were no longer alone in the universe, and nothing would ever be the same again whether he liked it or not. It would turn the whole world upside down.

The news report continued with dozens of experts speculating on the arrival of the spaceships and what type of life-forms might be inside them. Mia learned there were clusters of ships in remote areas of Scotland, Cumberland and Wales, as well as hundreds of other confirmed locations throughout the world. In total, seventeen thousand of the alien craft were known about, with an untold number likely to be still unreported in third-world countries. Of the known locations, all of them were now surrounded by military, but so far none of the attempts to communicate via any radio frequency had been successful.

Later in the night, news came in that the Soviet Union had launched nuclear warheads at a landing site in Siberia. The bombs had devastated the surrounding area, but didn't seem to cause any visible damage to the spacecraft themselves. This action was met with consternation from the United Nations, but that didn't stop other countries following the Russian lead, with the same results.

Richard Nixon, president of the United States of America, called an emergency meeting between world leaders to tackle the problem, and Prime Minister Edward Heath was flown out to America to attend. An endless stream of military and political commentators speculated on what possible solutions they might come up with to deal with any potential reprisals from the aliens.

When the bell rang to signal closing time, nobody watching the television took any notice of it. They were too engrossed in the continuing news broadcast, and didn't want to miss anything that might happen with the mysterious flying saucers. Dirk frowned. Basher toyed with his knife, while others sat with their arms folded and glared at the backs of the citizens standing before the television.

Mia and a few of the other men and women of Satan's Bastards headed for the toilets to empty their bladders while they had the chance. Once all the regular customers left it would be time for the party to start proper. Except they didn't seem to be in any particular hurry to go, and the bar staff weren't doing anything about it either. They were all staring at the TV screen too.

Bonehead stood by the pool table with a cue in his hand, while Tanner loaded the white ball into a sock and spun it around his wrist. Mia grinned at them as she passed by on the way to the toilet, the adrenalin rush already surging through her. They were still there when she returned. As were all the people standing around the television.

"Shouldn't they be going home by now?" she asked.

Bonehead grunted. "Sod this," he said, and strode over to the television with the pool cue in one hand. He shoved his way through the crowd gathered around it, bent down, and pulled out the plug. The TV image shrank to a tiny white dot in the centre of the screen, then faded away to nothing.

"Hey, put it back on," someone demanded. Others around him murmured in agreement.

Bonehead glared at them all in turn as he raised the pool cue in both hands. "Show's over, now piss off."

Dirk and Deano joined Bonehead by the television. Dirk grabbed a young Bowie by the shirt collar and bundled him through the door, sending him on his way with a shove to the back that sent him sprawling into the street. Deano swung a punch at another man and split his bottom lip. The man howled and ran for the door, blood pouring down his shirt. More bikers stepped forward, fists clenched. Spanners and chains appeared from inside leather jackets. Basher raised his knife like a dagger.

The more intelligent customers weighed up their options and hurried for the exit. Others had to be more forcefully ejected, but eventually Satan's Bastards had the pub to themselves. Dirk bolted the door behind the last of the stragglers and turned to face the bar staff, who were staring at him, wide-eyed.

"What the hell is this?" the barmaid asked. "You'd better get out now, or I'm calling the police."

Wicked Tina pulled a dagger from her motorcycle boot and

waved it at the barmaid. "I'd suggest you rethink that, honey."

Dirk cracked his knuckles and smiled. "I'd do what the lady asks, if I were you."

Several bikers took off their studded wristbands and wrapped them around their knuckles as they wandered over. Tanner joined them, and made a point of swinging the sock with the pool ball inside it down on the bar so the staff would know how much damage it could do to their skulls if they didn't behave.

Then Basher and Dirk swarmed behind the bar and grabbed the two barmen. One struggled and got a punch in the face from Dirk that knocked him out cold. The other looked down at his feet as he was marched over to the pool table by Basher and forced to sit beside one of its legs while Wicked Tina secured him to it with a ball of string she carried for that very purpose. Dirk and Deano took a leg each of the unconscious man and dragged him over so he could be tied next to him.

The barmaid watched it all with wide, staring eyes, her mouth hanging open. She raised her hands and flinched away when Fat Brenda squeezed her way behind the bar and headed straight for her.

"Why are you doing this?" she asked, her voice high-pitched and squeaky.

"Because we can," Fat Brenda said with a shrug. "And because we want to."

The woman snatched up an empty beer bottle from the bar and waved it at Fat Brenda by the stem in one shaking hand. "Don't come any closer," she warned.

Fat Brenda gave out a snort of derision and grabbed her by the hair, then twisted it until she screamed and dropped the bottle. She continued screaming and flailing her arms all the way over to the pool table, and refused to sit down so she could be tied up with the two men. Fat Brenda punched her in the stomach and she crumpled with a gasp. Dirk and Basher grasped her hands and secured them behind her back while Wicked Tina tied her to a leg of the pool table.

"Look," Mia said to the barmaid softly, "we don't want to hurt you any more than we already have. If you behave, you'll be fine and we'll let you go in the morning."

"Yeah," Wicked Tina said, holding up her dagger. "Or we could do it the hard way instead, if that's what you prefer.

Your choice, honey, it makes no difference to us."

With the bar staff all secured, bikers helped themselves to drinks while Dirk opened up the till and took out all the banknotes, then stuffed them into his leather jacket.

Skinny Brenda plugged in the jukebox and Gary Glitter warbled back to full speed. Wicked Tina raided the till for the loose change Dirk had left in it and fed coins into the jukebox, choosing songs at random. Fat Brenda, Suzy and Skinny Brenda danced with her while the bar staff watched on in absolute terror from their seated position.

By midnight several bikers had passed out drunk and lay slumped against the bar or splayed out on the benches while Margot and Randy Mandy drew cocks and balls on their foreheads with black marker pens. Bonehead staggered around with a pint glass filled with a lethal concoction of whisky, vodka and Pernod, spilling more down himself than he managed to tip into his mouth.

Fat Brenda stood on the pool table, stripped down to her knickers and motorcycle boots. A bottle of vodka in one hand, she swung her arms and stamped her feet to Slade's Cum on Feel the Noize as she shouted along with the chorus. Dirk cheered her on, watching Fat Brenda's ample rolls of fat jiggle and her huge breasts with Dirk's mark of ownership tattooed beneath the nipple of each one swing from side to side.

Tanner and Wicked Tina copulated on the floor, while the barmaid watched with mounting horror. Mia wanted to reassure her she was in no danger, that the bikers hated rapists as much as anyone else, but she doubted the woman would believe her after what she had already been through. It would all be over soon enough anyway, then she could go back to her usual, mundane existence with an exciting story to tell.

Mia drained her beer bottle and slammed it down on the table, then stumbled to her feet and staggered over to the television. While nobody else seemed the slightest bit interested in the alien spacecraft, and had probably forgotten all about them by now, Mia wanted to see if there were any new developments before she found somewhere to crash for the night. She crouched down and picked up the plug, then slid it around the wall socket for a few seconds before she managed to insert it. The television's sound came on instantly.

"... a momentous period in our history, one we are all very

fortunate to share on this day. Words cannot describe how exciting this is for me ..." It was Patrick Moore again, speaking very fast.

Mia lurched across the sticky wooden flooring and sat down cross-legged to peer up at the television. The image slowly faded into view, and Patrick Moore stared down at her through his monocle.

"... just to be a witness to our first encounter with extraterrestrial life is extraordinary. And just think of all we can learn from them once we understand their means of communication."

The television broadcast cut to a still image of ... something. Mia covered one eye and stared up at it, trying to bring it into focus. It was pure white, with an elongated body that looked like it had been stretched out of shape. It had long, spindly legs, and very long arms with three appendages on each that ended in what looked like the suckers of an octopus's tentacles. It seemed to be naked, but there was no sign of any sexual organs. Its head too was elongated, and came to a dull point at its tip. One huge black eye formed most of what could be termed its face, with a small round opening below it that may have been a mouth.

"The similarities to our own physiology are truly remarkable," Patrick Moore continued in voiceover. "It's astonishing to think how closely their evolution must have mirrored ours. And the technological advances they must have made just to reach our solar system are quite simply mind boggling."

"Now that is one ugly bastard," Bonehead said as he sat down on the floor beside Mia. "If I ever meet one of them things out on the road I'm going to poke it in the eye and see how loud it squeals."

7

The mechanical kerthunk of a motorcycle being kick-started came from beyond the clearing, closely followed by the guttural roar of an engine revving. Mia looked up sharply and locked eyes with Margot, who was sitting on the opposite side of the mass grave.

"Where the hell's she going?" Margot asked, rising to her feet. "She knows better than to ride out in the day."

Suzy shrugged. "Maybe she's just clearing out the pipes and shit?"

After another couple of revs the motorcycle dropped into first gear with a clunk and set off down the dirt track. Mia swore and jumped to her feet, ran to the edge of the clearing and dived through the bushes just in time to see Fat Brenda disappear around a bend.

"FB, wait!" Mia shouted. She turned to Margot, who had followed her through the bushes. "What should we do?"

Margot frowned. "Go after her, see what she's playing at. But watch out for any Angels, and don't lead them back here if they spot you."

Mia nodded, then climbed on her bike and kick-started it. She set off down the dirt track with her feet dangling and dabbed her way onto the tarmac road. Fat Brenda already had a big lead, and had almost reached the exit gate when Mia opened up the throttle. Fat Brenda turned right onto the main road and roared away into the distance. Mia accelerated up to sixty, waiting until the last moment before she braked hard to take the junction in pursuit.

The main road was mostly straight with gentle curves, and Mia was able to get up to ninety with ease as she sped past the wrecked and burnt out cars. Fat Brenda's brake light flashed as she navigated a roundabout at speed, taking a racing line through it. Mia sounded her horn, hoping it would remind Fat Brenda of the risk she was taking riding in daylight, but to no avail. She took the same racing line through the roundabout as Fat Brenda had and pushed her bike harder, desperate to close the gap before they were both spotted by an Angel patrol.

They raced on, both bike engines screaming in protest as they hurtled past farmland and brown fields. Mia gained a little ground on the straights, and got close enough to recognise the bike Fat Brenda rode as Dirk's Royal Enfield Interceptor. No wonder she had struggled to keep up; thanks to Dirk's fine-tuning it was the fastest bike any of them owned, and could out-accelerate anything on the road, even the newer Japanese super-bikes. For Mia to have made any headway at all Fat Brenda must have been holding back on some of its power.

Another roundabout came up in the distance. Fat Brenda's brake light came on as she approached a sign detailing where each of the five branching roads led to. Mia saw her chance and took it. She twisted the throttle savagely and pulled alongside her, then eased off as she forced Fat Brenda over to the side of the road. Fat Brenda came to a halt and stared straight ahead. Mia parked her bike diagonally in front of her so she couldn't get away again, and climbed off. She straddled Fat Brenda's front wheel and reached over the handlebars to switch the engine off.

"Where are you going, FB?" she asked softly.

Fat Brenda's cheeks glistened with tears. "Scotland," she said, and wiped her nose with the sleeve of her leather jacket.

"What are you going there for?" Mia asked.

"You know what for."

Mia nodded. "I reckon I can guess. But do you think this is what Dirk would have wanted? You going off on some half-arsed suicide mission and getting yourself killed? You think any of them would have wanted that?"

"Dirk would have wanted revenge if it was me they'd killed."

"I get it, FB, I really do. I want to see those bastards pay for what they've done too, but if it was that easy the army would've wiped them out as soon as they attacked, wouldn't they? Christ, Russia dropped atom bombs on them, and look what good that did. You really think you can take them out with a piddly little shotgun? You'd get yourself killed long before you got anywhere near them."

Fat Brenda shrugged. "Yeah well, you think I care about

that? It's my fault they all died, I brought those alien bastards over here when I wrecked my bike. If it wasn't for me they'd all still be alive right now. So as long as I take some of those bug-eyed freaks with me, I don't care what happens after that. This is something I've got to do, and you're not going to talk me out of it no matter what you say, so you might as well just piss off back to the others and leave me to it."

Mia sighed. "Okay, okay, I get it. And there's nothing I want more than to go with you and wipe some of those bastards out. But not like this. It needs planning first. Remember that feud we had with those Romanian bikers over in Chesterfield, The Warlords or whatever it was they called themselves? You think that would have gone down so well if we'd just steamed in without any preparation? They would've just picked us off one by one as soon as they saw us coming."

"Yeah well, maybe. But it was Tanner who always did the planning, and he can't help us this time, can he?"

Fat Brenda sniffled, then wiped a tear away angrily. Mia placed a hand on the woman's bicep and nodded sympathetically.

"I know it was, that was Tanner's job and he was very good at it. But when it's just us and the other women out on the supply runs? We all have a say in what to do when we get into a bit of bother, and we always manage to pull through okay, don't we? We can do that now, take our time and plan it all out properly so we can do it right, cause as much damage to them as we can, then get the hell out of there. So what do you say? Let's give the others a chance to come with us, yeah? They've lost just as much as we have, so let's involve them too. But either way, we do it right, yeah? No running off half-cocked, and no bloody suicide missions."

Fat Brenda frowned, then nodded. "Yeah, okay."

They turned their bikes around and rode back to the nature reserve together. A small part of Mia hoped Fat Brenda would eventually forget about revenge, or that Margot, Suzy and Wicked Tina would manage to talk her out of it. But the rest of her looked forward to taking out as many of those alien bastards as she could.

PART 2
THE JOURNEY NORTH

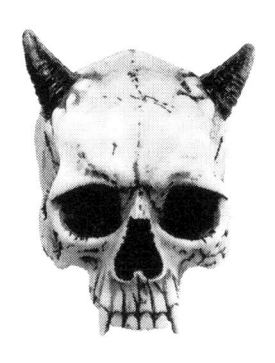

8

Mia pushed a shopping trolley loaded with empty petrol cans down the scorched and pock-marked road, avoiding the craters as she followed Suzy down the town's high street. Finding fuel was easy enough, although it was always a risk venturing out in the day, and they had to keep one eye on the sky at all times, just in case. Rusting cars and vans littered the road in disarray, like a huge, abandoned dodgem track. Many vehicles still held the desiccated corpses of drivers and passengers, their metal tombs protecting them from scavenging wildlife. Others, their windscreens shattered on impact with lamp posts, buildings and other solid objects, held little more than bones and scraps of clothing. Those were ignored in favour of the ones with no inhabitants, because neither of them wanted to risk touching the rotting corpses in case they carried any diseases.

Huge swarms of flies buzzed everywhere, and Mia had to constantly swat them away from her face as she walked. But it was the smell that was the worst. Countless thousands of decomposing bodies trapped in the rubble of houses and shops, factories and warehouses. The putrescence drifting up from open sewers stuffed with the remains of fleeing victims who thought they could find safety underground. Even with nose-plugs in place, a wet bandana covering her mouth, Mia could taste that smell in the back of her throat. She would never get used to that stench, no matter how much time she spent in the towns and cities of the dead.

It had been three days since they left the nature reserve for the last time, their bikes loaded up with supplies for the long trek north. The decision to leave had been unanimous, arrived at within minutes of Fat Brenda stating her case for revenge. That just left the small detail of how they were going to go about putting it into practice, when the whole world's military had failed so miserably. But, as Fat Brenda reasoned, they could figure that out when they got there. They'd picked up new sleeping bags along the way, and slept during the daylight hours so they could ride all night. The further north they travelled, the harder Fat Brenda pushed them, only allowing them to stop to rest when Angel ships flew close enough to spot them.

Suzy picked up a brick and shattered the driver side window of a green Morris Oxford, then reached inside for the car's keys. Mia pushed the shopping trolley over while Suzy unlocked the petrol cap and peered inside with a torch.

"Any good?" Mia asked, waving a swarm of flies away from her face.

"Yeah, there's a bit in there. Not much though."

Suzy pulled a plastic tube from inside her leather jacket, then fed one end of it into the car's petrol tank and sucked on the other to siphon off the fuel. She only managed to fill up two of the empty petrol cans before the car's tank ran dry, then moved on in search of another uninhabited vehicle while Mia pushed the shopping trolley behind her.

A church stood on the corner of the next street they came to, its grounds filled with gnawed skeletons wearing muddy rags, the remains of hundreds of people hoping to atone for their sins in the last few minutes of their lives. Rats, no longer afraid to surface during the day, scurried across the yellowing bones in search of any meat left behind by earlier generations. The church's door had been chewed through, and a constant river of glistening black bodies flowed in and out of it. This was their world now, and countless pairs of eyes glowered at Mia and Suzy as they walked by, as if they were daring them to enter their domain.

Another street, another jumble of wrecked cars filled with decaying bodies. In this town, it looked to Mia like everyone had the same idea to escape by road. She wanted to believe some of them had got away before the roads became saturated and impassable, before the Angels arrived to finish them off, but she knew it was unlikely the warning had come in time. There were no survivors hiding out in the countryside, like Satan's Bastards had been. If there were, they would have seen some trace of them by now. The world was dead. Mia, Suzy, Wicked Tina, Margot and Fat Brenda were probably the only ones left out of the whole of humanity.

Mia had to wrestle the shopping trolley onto the pavement when she found her way blocked by several burnt-out cars, while Suzy simply vaulted onto the bonnet of the nearest one and walked over its roof to jump down at the other side. Beyond the wreckage sat dozens more cars, bumper to bumper, taking up both sides of the road. Car doors hung open, the vehicles abandoned by their drivers and passengers when they could go no further. Suzy checked the petrol tanks of each empty vehicle, and they filled up another four cans before moving on.

As they walked, a yellow Austin Allegro caught Mia's eye and she stopped to look at it more closely. She felt a sudden flash of recognition, but couldn't quite work out why. She had never been to this town before, didn't even know the name of it, so she certainly wouldn't know the owners, and it was unlikely she had ever seen the car before. Yet the feeling of familiarity persisted.

Suzy stopped at a Morris Minor on the opposite side of the road and twisted off the petrol cap. Mia parked the shopping trolley next to her and walked over to the Austin Allegro to inspect it more closely. She peered through its windscreen. The remains of a woman in a flowery summer dress grinned out at her from the passenger seat. Her head had flopped to one side and rested on the window, its sunken, sightless eyes staring out. In the driver seat sat another corpse, this one a bearded man wearing blue denim jeans and a faded Bob Dylan T-shirt. The bodies were too decomposed to make out any features, and she couldn't estimate their age, but Mia knew instinctively it wasn't them who had triggered the memory.

It was the car itself.

She glanced down at the black and silver number plate below the radiator grill, hoping it would spark some memory. When nothing came she shook her head and continued around the car, pausing to look through the rear side window. The remnants of two young children lay slumped on the rear seat, sandwiched by large brown suitcases either side of them. A black and white dog lay between them, its head hanging down over the edge of the seat, its long since dried up tongue lolling from its open mouth.

Mia gasped. The ground seemed to lurch to one side, and she had to reach out for the car to steady herself. Suddenly she knew. Her parents owned a car just like this one. Same make, same model, same colour.

Mia was four years old, and it was time for the annual family holiday in Skegness. She could remember it like it was yesterday. The overwhelming excitement she felt at the prospect of a whole week staying at Butlins. No work to take her parents away from her, no daycare to go to, just endless hours of sun, sand and play to look forward to. The journey down the motorway, trundling along behind a convoy of lorries in the slow lane. Summer Holiday playing on the radio, everyone competing to see who could sing along the loudest. Her dog, Prince, barking along too, as if he knew the words and wanted to join in the fun with his own doggy version. Her baby sister Gemma gurgling happily in her lap.

Then her mother screamed, and the car lurched to one side. Her father screamed too. Prince barked. Gemma cried. The world outside the car began to spin. Then Gemma flew out of her hands and Mia shot forward and hit her head on something and blacked out.

She woke to the sound of wailing sirens and grinding metal, showers of sparks cascading down on her. Her head hurt, and she could feel something warm and slimy trickling down her face. The car's roof floated away and giant hands reached down to pluck her from where she lay on the floor of the car, in the small gap between the front and rear seats.

"Close your eyes, darling," a voice said. "Don't look."

Mia looked anyway.

And screamed.

"Mia? What is it? What's wrong?"

Mia looked up through her tears. She blinked, surprised to find herself sat on the tarmac, leaning against the side of the yellow car and hugging her knees. Suzy stood over her, looking down in concern. Mia shook her head and tried to wipe away the tears, but they kept on coming.

"I had a baby sister," she said between sobs. "Gemma. How could I have forgotten? Oh god, I think I killed her."

"What are you going on about?"

"I can remember it all. My parents didn't abandon me, they died in a car crash. Gemma was on my knee, I was supposed to look after her but I didn't hold her tight enough. She ... she —"

Mia couldn't put it into words. Gemma's tiny body

crumpled over the gearstick, the top of her head caved in, her brains spilling out. She held her face and sobbed into her hands.

Suzy sat down on the ground next to Mia and placed an arm around her shoulders. Mia melted into her and sobbed harder. Suzy stroked her hair.

"Mia," she said softly, "you would've just been a kid yourself, there wouldn't have been anything you could do. What happened was bloody shitty, yeah, but you can't blame yourself for it. And there's no point dwelling on a past you can't change."

9

Life carried on as normal for Satan's Bastards during the two years the Angels lived in harmony with the Earth's population. They caught snippets of excited conversation about them on their travels, and saw them greeting world leaders on staged TV broadcasts when they stopped off at public houses, but even to Mia the novelty soon wore off and she hardly thought about them at all.

The weekend before the Angels attacked she was at Knebworth Festival, tripping on some acid Bonehead had scored, while Pink Floyd performed their new concept album, Angels Among Us. Centre stage, towering above the band, stood a huge, thirty-foot tall inflatable PVC Angel that swayed from side to side in time to the music. Its long arms waved in the air, while multi-coloured laser beams shot from each sucker of its elongated fingers to cascade around the night sky in a kaleidoscope of constantly swirling colours. Occasionally the Angel's legs would buckle as the compressed air holding it erect was cut off, and it would bow down over the audience as if it were reaching out to grab them before springing back up and resuming its dance once it was inflated again.

Mia stared at the PVC Angel, mesmerised by its motion while the music washed over her. In her drug-addled mind the band seemed to turn into skeletons before her eyes as they danced around the alien like a maypole, the cables trailing from their instruments turning into red ribbons that wound around the Angel's legs to bind it.

Fat Brenda swayed by Mia's side, mimicking the movements of the Angel precisely while she sang along to a completely different song to the one the band on stage were playing. Dirk, Bonehead and Tanner sat cross-legged on the ground before her, their heads bowed, staring at the buckles on their motorcycle boots and giggling. The horned skulls painted on the back of their leather jackets seemed to sparkle and shimmer in the evening gloom. Wicked Tina, naked from the waist up, sat on Basher's shoulders, swinging her arms around madly while Basher clung onto her motorcycle boots to stop her toppling off him.

After the festival ended they all retired to their tents in a nearby field and came down from their acid trips with the assistance of copious amounts of cannabis and barbiturates washed down with cider, eventually passing out just after dawn. They slept through the day and into the following night. At one point Mia woke to find herself naked, with Bonehead pressing down on top of her, suckling at her breasts. She raked her fingernails down his bare back and raised her knees, then reached down to guide his penis inside her. After he finished he rolled onto his back and Mia traced her index finger up and down the scythe of the grim reaper figure tattooed on his chest until he fell asleep.

The next morning they rolled up their tents and sleeping bags and stashed them on the back of their motorcycles with bungee clips ready for the road. Word had spread among the crowd at Knebworth there was a top secret music festival in Derbyshire the following weekend, with American band Lynyrd Skynyrd headlining. Support bands were said to include Hawkwind, Gong, Slade and T-Rex, and there would be free magic mushroom tea and marihuana cakes for everyone who attended. Nobody seemed to know precisely where the festival was to be held or who was organising it, and Mia wasn't entirely convinced the rumours were true, but nobody wanted to take the risk of missing out on what sounded like the event of the year. So the decision was made to head north in search of further information.

They eschewed the M1 in favour of a more scenic route along B roads through Stevenage and Letchworth, eventually stopping for dinner in a small village called Moggerhanger because Dirk liked the sound of its name and wanted to see what it had to offer. Which was nothing of interest, as it turned out, and after a quick meal and a few pints in the village's one and only pub, followed by a bit of fun with the local country bumpkins, they moved on through Kettering and Corby into Nottinghamshire.

Riding down a B road cutting through the countryside, Mia took the lead on her Norton Commando. Having grown up in

Retford she knew the area better than anyone else, and had acquaintances in nearby Rotherham who might know where the festival was to be held. Wicked Tina followed close behind on her Honda 350, with Bonehead, Suzy, Fat Brenda and Basher riding in single file behind. Next came Dirk, followed by Tanner, Stevo, Skinny Brenda and the rest, a long convoy of motorcycles trailing back almost half a mile.

Mia followed the signs to Rotherham and turned off onto an A road leading into the town. She soon came to a roundabout with four junctions, and slowed on the approach to it while she glanced to her right to check for oncoming traffic. The junction was clear, and she joined the roundabout without stopping.

Then her peripheral vision registered something approaching at high speed from the left. She spun her head toward it just as Wicked Tina hit the brakes and shouted a warning. A grey car headed straight for Mia, the driver seemingly oblivious to her existence as he entered the roundabout. Too late to brake herself, Mia did the only thing she could do and twisted the throttle as far as it would go. The bike surged forward with a roar. Mia had to bank over hard so she could navigate her way around the roundabout, and took the first exit cursing the driver for not looking where he was going.

Then came a sickening crunch of metal impacting metal behind her, followed by a thud and the tinkle of shattering glass and plastic. Mia slammed on the brakes with a feeling of dread in her heart. She dived off her bike and ran back to the roundabout.

One of the bikes lay on its side, its rider lying face down in the road nearby. The other bikers had parked haphazardly across the roundabout, blocking off all the approaches, and stood circled around the car, a grey Ford Cortina with a crumpled bonnet. The driver of the car, a young man in his mid-twenties with long brown hair, stared out of the cracked windscreen in shock, his hands gripping the steering wheel tight. Mia concentrated on the faces of the bikers as they took their helmets off, ticking their names off in her mind.

"Bonehead!" she shouted when she realised who the fallen biker was, and rushed over to him with Wicked Tina.

"I'm okay," Bonehead said as they helped him to his feet.

"But that bastard soon won't be."

Bonehead brushed gravel off his scuffed leather trousers and stormed over to the car with his fists clenched. The driver had got out, and held up his hands while he pleaded with the other bikers.

"I didn't see him," he said, his voice high-pitched, his eyes wide and staring. "He came from nowhere, there was nothing I could do." The bikers stood in silence before him, arms folded. The man avoided their steely gaze. "Look, I don't want any trouble, I'll pay for the damage." He took out a wallet and flipped it open. "I've got thirty pounds on me, but I can get more if you need it."

Something in the bikers' stare, or some kind of sixth sense, must have warned the man about his imminent danger because he spun around just before Bonehead reached him. He dropped his wallet and backed away, palms out.

"Sorry mate, I didn't see you," he stammered.

"Yeah?" Bonehead said, closing the gap in three more strides. "Well you can see me now, right?"

Bonehead took off his open-face helmet and swung it left-handed by the strap at the side of the man's head. The man howled and clutched his ear. Bonehead punched him in the stomach with his right fist, and as he doubled over he grabbed his hair and jerked his head down to meet the reinforced kneepad he raised at the same time. The man howled again and fell onto his arse, clasping his bloody nose and mouth. He whimpered, his shoulders shaking. Bonehead stepped up to him and kicked him in the face, knocking him onto his back. His hands fell to the sides and his eyes rolled up in their sockets. Bonehead was about to stamp on his chest when Dirk stopped him.

"That's enough, Bonehead, go and check your bike."

Bonehead looked up and nodded, then gave the driver's body one last kick and walked over to his motorcycle. Mia helped him get it upright and kicked down the side-stand to rest it on. They both walked around it, inspecting the damage. It had a lot more dents and scratches than it had before, and the wing mirror and indicator on the right hand side were both smashed, but other than that it was just superficial. A small amount of petrol had leaked from the carburettor, and Mia pointed this out in warning when she saw Bonehead take out his cigarettes.

Dozens of flying saucers zipped overhead in a V formation. Mia looked up to watch them pass and wondered where they were heading. She saw RAF jets following them, and assumed they were all heading to some outdoor air display event close by, most likely at Finningley, near Doncaster. When she looked back down Bonehead was walking away from her, heading for the car. Basher held out a spare motorcycle chain he carried in his toolbox for emergencies, and Bonehead took it from him. He doubled it over and swung it at the car's windscreen, shattering it into hundreds of tiny pieces that cascaded over the seats inside. He smashed the headlights and indicators, walked around to the rear of the car and did the same to those lights, then started on the car's side windows and bodywork. Basher took out his flick-knife and joined in by slashing the car's tyres and ripping up the seats.

Then something exploded in the distance.

Wicked Tina gaped at Mia. "What the hell's that?"

Mia shrugged. "Dunno."

Somewhere close by, people started screaming.

"Let's go check it out," Dirk said. He inserted two fingers in his mouth and whistled. When Bonehead and Basher turned to look he waved them over. "Your bike okay to ride?" he asked Bonehead. Bonehead nodded. "Let's go then."

The screams grew louder as they rode into the outskirts of Rotherham and parked up on the brow of a hill leading down to a housing estate. Mia caught a whiff of something in the air, and tasted something metallic in her mouth, a tingling sensation on her tongue like licking the contacts of a battery. She stared, wide-eyed and open-mouthed at the crazy scene before her.

A huge mob ran through the streets, shouting and flailing their arms. Some fell, and were trampled underfoot by those following them. A car's engine gunned somewhere behind them, then tore down the road and ploughed into the crowd, sending bodies flying in all directions. It hit a lamp post and the driver shot through the windscreen to land in a bloody heap on the car's bonnet.

In the distance, buildings were burning. A car exploded, the force of the blast raising it off the ground before it tumbled back down on its side, then rolled onto its roof engulfed in flames. People within the running crowd clutched their throats and fell to their knees, their eyes bulging. Others ran past them, uncaring, until they too fell. Above it all hung an Angel ship, hovering half a mile above the ground, narrow blue beams of light shooting from it in all directions, destroying everything they touched. Buildings crumbled and fell. Cars and vans exploded. Twitching bodies blackened and burned. Nothing survived the Angels' wave of destruction.

The other bikers were climbing on their motorcycles and kick-starting them, but Mia was hardly aware of their existence as she continued watching in grim fascination. A man stumbled out of a side street, holding what looked like a wet tea towel over his mouth. One of the blue laser beams struck him in the chest and he burst into flames and pitched forward, then fell silently to his knees before toppling over. She watched his skin blister and crack, watched his body burst open, then blacken and smoulder.

A hand grabbed Mia's arm. She startled and spun around, her fist rising instinctively to lash out.

"Come on!" Bonehead shouted, and dragged her to her bike.

10

Suzy helped Mia get the shopping trolley up a ramp leading to the first floor of the multi-storey car park the women had chosen to sleep in for the day. Fat Brenda sat by herself, leaning against a stone pillar, staring down at her motorcycle boots. She looked miserable, but that was understandable enough. They all were, and the thought of revenge was the only thing keeping them going.

Mia pushed the trolley over to the bikes, her mind still filled with visions of the horrific death of her parents and baby sister. But the fact her parents had loved her after all, and hadn't just abandoned her at that awful foster home like she had always assumed, was a small comfort she could cling to.

Fat Brenda, meanwhile, had nothing to lift her spirits. While they were inactive like this she just moped around, wallowing in misery. Mia had hoped the woman would snap out of it once they left the nature reserve and hit the road, but that hadn't been the case. If anything it had made her worse, more impatient for revenge and angry about how long it was all taking. She snapped at them constantly, as if it were their fault they had to stay put during the day.

Wicked Tina and Margot strapped their rolled up sleeping bags on the back of their bikes with bungee clips, then turned to wave when they saw Mia approach with the shopping trolley. They took petrol cans from the trolley and filled up their bikes, then loaded spares into their saddle-bags. Fat Brenda didn't budge from her position by the stone pillar, so Mia filled up her bike for her after she'd rolled up her sleeping bag and stashed it on the back of her Norton.

She opened up one of the saddle-bags and took out a pair of binoculars, then walked over to the edge of the car park and looked out into the distance. It didn't take long to find what she was looking for — a clutch of Angel ships all heading north in the same direction. She followed their position with the binoculars as they hovered across the rapidly darkening sky and disappeared over the horizon, then returned to her bike.

"Well?" Wicked Tina asked. "Have they gone?"

"Yeah," Mia said as she put the binoculars back in the saddle-bag. "Time to go."

Fat Brenda looked up and struggled to her feet. Without saying a word, she rolled up her sleeping bag and fastened it to the back of her bike.

"You okay, FB?" Mia asked.

Fat Brenda nodded, then climbed on her bike and kick-started it. She revved its engine to warm it up, then pulled forward. Mia and the others followed in procession, across the car park, down the ramp, and out onto the road. They weaved their way around abandoned vehicles and soon came to a B road leading out of the town and back into the countryside.

Hordes of flying night-time insects battered against Mia's face as she picked up speed and banked into a gentle curve. Yellow splatters appeared on the lenses of her goggles, obscuring her vision. She wiped them away with her left thumb, smearing them across the glass, only for them to be replaced by more kamikaze insects mere seconds later. She eased off on the throttle, dropped down a gear, and followed the faint outline of the other bikes.

They rode on for another two hours, until they came to a hump-backed bridge crossing a river. Wicked Tina, who had taken the lead at the time, came to a halt on the approach to the bridge and climbed off her bike.

"What've you stopped for?" Fat Brenda said as she pulled up alongside her.

"Are you kidding, honey? We've been riding for ages, and my arse is numb. Besides, I need a piss."

Fat Brenda frowned. "We don't have time for that, we've got a lot of distance to cover tonight."

Mia parked her bike behind them and dismounted. "She's right, FB, we can't ride all night without a break again, it pretty much crippled us last night. We need to stretch our legs every couple of hours or so, otherwise they'll just seize up."

Fat Brenda grunted. "Yeah well, you'd better hurry up or I'm going on my own." She revved her bike's engine, then glared at Wicked Tina's back as she made her way down a grassy embankment to the river's edge.

Suzy and Margot stepped off their bikes and walked onto the bridge, stopping in the middle to lean against a stone wall. Margot took out a pack of cigarettes and offered one to Suzy. Suzy took it and lit it with her Zippo lighter, cupping her hand over the flame. She held out the lit cigarette for Margot to light hers from, then leaned over the wall and gazed down at the river while they both smoked.

Mia took off her goggles and inspected them under the glow of her headlight. The lenses were encrusted with bits of insects, which she tried to flick off without much success. She wiped her forehead and found more insect remains on her fingers, and decided to join Wicked Tina down at the river to rinse herself down.

"You should stretch your legs too," Mia said to Fat Brenda.

Fat Brenda didn't reply, but as Mia made her way down the embankment she heard her switch her bike's engine off, and assumed she had decided to take her advice. Down at the river, Wicked Tina stripped off and placed her clothes on nearby rocks. She waded into the running water naked, her teeth chattering, then sat down in the centre of the river and splashed water over herself.

Mia wasn't that brave. She crouched down at the edge of the river and rinsed the insects off her goggles, then scooped up handfuls of water to wash her face. The water was freezing, so she could only imagine how cold Wicked Tina must be.

"You two finished pissing about yet?" Fat Brenda shouted down from the top of the bridge. She had joined Suzy and Margot up there, and all three of them leaned over the wall to watch Wicked Tina splash around like a kid in a paddling pool from the light of a torch held by Suzy.

"Yeah, just about," Mia shouted back. "Tina, it's time to go."

Wicked Tina raised a thumb and stood up, shook herself like a wet dog, then turned to the far embankment and looked up.

"Angels!" she shouted, and threw herself flat in the water with a big splash.

Mia dived to the ground and flattened herself against it. She heard Fat Brenda swear, then the sound of motorcycle boots running across the bridge. The ground began to vibrate.

The sky filled with an iridescent blue hue. Mia clasped her hands over her ears, trying to block out the deafening drone vibrating through her skull. She knew the Angel ship was close, that instant death might be only a matter of seconds away, and closed her eyes. She lay as still as she could, hardly daring to breathe, wondering if she would feel anything when the laser beams shot down and incinerated her. She screwed up her face and clenched her fists in readiness.

The flying saucer thundered overhead. A shockwave rocked Mia's body and flattened plants around her. A wave of ice-cold water splashed over her and took her breath away. The humming diminished, then faded away to nothing. Mia raised her head and looked up. Suzy held out a hand to help her to her feet.

"Now that was bloody close," Suzy said, grinning down.

"It would've been a lot worse if we hadn't stopped for a piss break, honey," Wicked Tina said, wading out of the river. She glared at Fat Brenda. "Then they would've caught us out on the road."

"Yeah well," Fat Brenda said, frowning, "it's gone now, and we've already wasted enough time. So get dressed and get back on your bike. We've got a job to do, remember? We don't have time to mess around like this anymore."

"Soz, boss," Wicked Tina said, bending down to pick up her motorcycle boots. Her leather jacket lay nearby, but the rest of her clothes had blown up the embankment and scattered across it.

Fat Brenda wheeled on her. "I mean it, Tina. The fun times are over, and the sooner you get that into your thick head the better."

"Piss off, you're not the boss of me."

Fat Brenda stepped toward Wicked Tina, her fists clenched. Mia blocked her path and raised a hand to ward her off.

"Look, both of you calm down, okay? Tina's right, if we hadn't stopped we'd have been toast by now. So let's just leave it at that and get going instead of wasting even more time arguing about it."

"There is another thing to consider," Suzy said. Everyone turned to look at her. "What are those bastards doing out at night? You usually only see them at night when something's caught their attention. So if it wasn't us, who the bloody hell was it?"

11

The women rode through a patch of torrential rain during the night, Fat Brenda having refused to stop to find shelter, and reached the outskirts of another town cold, exhausted and wet just before dawn. The name of the town didn't matter to Mia, and she barely glanced at its welcome sign as she passed it by. All towns were the same now. Some were bigger than others, but that just meant they held more rotting corpses. They were somewhere in Northumberland, at a guess, having already passed through South and then North Yorkshire.

The rain had turned into a light drizzle when Fat Brenda gave the signal to halt at the top of a hill leading down to the town centre. They pulled up beside a lone, two-story Victorian house on the left hand side of the road. A large, grassy woodland area fenced off by a dry-stone wall stood on the opposite side.

Mia climbed off her bike and arched her aching back. Bikes were never designed for travelling long distances without a break, even in fair weather. Her arse was numb from spending too much time in the saddle, and she needed to get out of her wet clothes, give them a chance to dry out before the next evening's ride.

She looped her goggles over the bike's handlebars and looked longingly at the house, wondering if that was where Fat Brenda planned to spend the night. There would be fresh clothes inside to change into, beds to sleep in. Maybe they could even gather some wood and get a fire going. Maybe even persuade Fat Brenda to put the journey on hold for a couple of days to let them all thaw out and recoup their energies. It wasn't as if the Angels were going anywhere, and they had all the time in the world to reach them. A few nights sleeping on real beds, or even just chairs and settees or a carpeted floor, would give them all a more than welcome break.

Wicked Tina took the shotgun from her leather jacket and

rested it on the seat of her motorcycle, then vaulted over the dry-stone wall and headed for one of the nearby trees. She dropped her jeans, squatted down with her back resting against the tree's trunk, and sighed as she urinated on the ground.

"Mia, pass me your binoculars," Fat Brenda said from astride her bike. Mia unfastened her saddle-bag and handed the binoculars to her. Fat Brenda cast them over the town centre in the shadowless pre-dawn light, then pointed. "There's a block of flats another mile or so down the road, they don't look like they've been damaged too much. I reckon that's as good a place as any to sleep."

Mia took the binoculars from Fat Brenda and looked through them. The block of flats, a twelve-story high-rise concrete building that would have once been home to hundreds of families, was scorched and cracked in places, but seemed to be structurally sound. It had a tall fence around its flat roof, no doubt to discourage suicide attempts, and a single large chimney in the centre with a huge TV aerial attached to it. The perfect vantage point for watching the Angels' nightly retreat. Mia nodded, then passed the binoculars to Suzy.

"Yeah, looks good to me," Suzy said, passing the binoculars to Margot after a cursory glance. Margot looked for herself, then gave the binoculars back to Mia.

Fat Brenda kicked her bike into gear and set off down the road, closely followed by Margot. Suzy climbed on her bike and waited while Mia returned the binoculars to the saddle-bag.

"Tina," Mia shouted, "time to go."

"Yeah, just a minute, honey," Wicked Tina shouted back. She pulled up her jeans and vaulted back over the wall.

"What the hell?" Suzy said.

"What?" Mia asked, glancing at Suzy. Suzy stared across at the woodland. Mia turned to follow her gaze, and her mouth dropped open. "Who the hell's that?"

A young boy, no more than six or seven years old, naked and covered in mud, stood crouched down on his hands and knees, sniffing the ground by the tree where Wicked Tina had urinated. He shuffled around in a semi-circle, his face close to the ground, then raised a leg and tried to piss against the tree. The urine dribbled down his leg instead, rinsing off some of the grime on his inner thigh.

"Hey," Wicked Tina called out to him. "Where did you come from?"

The boy looked up, clearly startled. He curled his lips back to reveal a set of uneven, yellowed teeth and gave out a high-pitched snarl. Mia walked up to the wall, her hands raised, palms out.

"It's okay, we're friends. Are your parents nearby?" Mia placed her hands on the wall's surface and leaned against it casually so she wouldn't alarm the boy any further. Suzy and Wicked Tina joined her, both staring at him.

The boy backed away on all fours, still showing his teeth, then sprang up onto his tiptoes and puffed out his chest. He gave out a sharp yelp, then turned and bolted away into the woodland.

"Hey, wait," Mia shouted after him, but the boy soon disappeared from view.

Suzy stared after him. "What do you reckon we should do?"

"Follow him," Mia said. "What else can we do? He's the first person we've seen for years, we can't just ignore him. There must be others round here somewhere, with a place that's safe enough to bring up children."

Wicked Tina shrugged. "Yeah well, even if there is it doesn't follow they'd take kindly to strangers sniffing around. Besides, wherever they are staying it must be pretty well hidden if they've managed to last this long. And that kid was filthy, it didn't look to me like anyone was taking care of it."

"All the more reason to go after him, then." Mia climbed onto the wall. There was a narrow drainage ditch on the other side, about a foot wide, and she hopped over it. She turned to face Suzy and Wicked Tina. "You two coming or not?"

Suzy swung a leg over the wall and straddled it, then shuffled herself across, jumping down into the ditch. Wicked Tina went back to her bike and retrieved the shotgun before vaulting over after them.

"What do you need that for?" Mia asked, pointing at the gun. "He's just a kid."

"Yeah well, it's not the kid I'm worried about, honey. It's his parents."

"What, so you're going to walk up to them waving a gun around? What sort of message is that going to send?"

"One that says don't mess with us."

Mia shook her head and sighed. "Christ, there's few enough of us left as it is, we should be reaching out to them in peace, not waving guns in their faces. It's not like the old days, we're all on the same side now."

"Yeah well, there's no harm in being prepared for trouble, just in case."

They set off through the wood together, wading through long wet grass and pushing through bracken. Damp twigs snapped beneath their motorcycle boots. Low branches whipped against their leather jackets.

"We're friends," Mia shouted, "we just want to talk to you."

"This is a waste of time," Wicked Tina said. "The kid's long gone."

Mia shook her head. "No, he's around here somewhere, he has to be."

"Not just him, either," Suzy said, pointing up. Seventeen flying saucers glided across the sky in a V formation, heading in their direction.

"Shit," Mia said, "that's all we need."

"We should've gone with Fat Brenda and Margot while we had the chance," Suzy said.

"Yeah well, it's too late now, honey. And we both know whose fault that is."

"Piss off, Tina," Mia said. "We couldn't just leave, not after we saw that kid."

"I don't see why not," Wicked Tina mumbled. "It's obvious he doesn't want anything to do with us."

They hid under the branches of a large tree until the Angel ships had flown over, then continued further into the woodland, soon coming to a small, grassed over clearing with a metal park bench at its centre. Small bones and tufts of bloody fur littered the grass around the bench. Mia could make out what looked like the skulls of rabbits amongst them, plus other small animals that may have been squirrels or large rats.

Mia was about to step into the clearing to take a closer look when she noticed an Angel ship hovering less than a mile away, high up in the sky. She pointed it out to the others, and directed them to skirt around the clearing, keeping undercover of a clump of trees circling it.

A low growl came from somewhere to Mia's left. She stopped and spun toward it, trying to pinpoint where the sound came from. The growl came again, from within a cluster of bushes. Suzy pointed. Mia looked closer. A pair of round black eyes stared out at her.

Mia and Suzy backed away as a large dog stepped out of the bushes, its yellow teeth bared. Its snout was bloody, with tufts of fur sticking to its maw. The dog looked old, with speckles of grey in its matted black fur, and unlike the younger dogs Mia was used to seeing roaming wild on the outskirts of towns, it wore a studded collar with a name-tag hanging from it.

Wicked Tina stood her ground and raised the shotgun. She aimed at the slowly approaching dog and curled her finger around the trigger.

Then the young boy ran out of the bush behind the dog, his hands stretched out before him like claws, his teeth bared.

"Stop, don't shoot!" Mia shouted.

Wicked Tina jerked the shotgun's barrel up just before she pulled the trigger. It boomed out, impossibly loud, and left Mia's ears ringing. Birds scattered from their perches with a thunderous flapping of wings as bits of leaves drifted down. Wicked Tina lost her balance and fell onto her back, losing her hold on the shotgun. It tumbled away from her and landed in the long wet grass nearby.

The boy gave out a series of short, yipping barks and pounced on Wicked Tina like a cat taking down its prey. His tiny fists flailed at her face as she stared up at him, wide-eyed and unbelieving. The dog crouched down on its haunches, growling and snarling.

Wicked Tina tried to prise the boy off her, but couldn't get a grip on the wet mud covering his body. Suzy rushed forward to help her and grabbed the boy around the waist, clasping her fingers together around his chest as she yanked him back. The boy wriggled himself free from her clutches and turned to face her. He barked, then lunged at her with his mouth wide open, his lips curled back. Suzy jerked her head back just in time and the boy's teeth clashed together inches away from her face. He snarled in frustration. Suzy backhanded him across the face and knocked him over, then straddled his chest to pin his arms to the ground.

The dog ran at Suzy, barking furiously. Mia ran to intercept it and barrelled into it shoulder-first just as it pounced, its jaws open wide to tear out Suzy's throat. The dog landed heavily on its side and yelped, then rolled over and scrabbled back to its feet. Mia stumbled and fell to her knees, unable to halt her forward momentum. The dog snarled and ran at her.

Mia raised her hands and braced herself. The dog pounced. Mia grabbed it around the throat with both hands as it flew toward her. Its weight knocked her onto her back, the dog on top. Bloody spittle flew from its mouth as it thrashed its head, its jaws snapping. Its breath smelled of rotting meat, and made Mia gag. She squeezed her fingers around the dog's neck, ignoring the studs on the collar that dug into her skin.

The dog's eyes bulged. It twisted its head wildly, trying to snap at Mia's wrists while its hind legs scrabbled at her waist. Sharp claws scratched through her denim jeans and sent shockwaves of pain through her body. The dog's mouth opened wide. A rasping snarl came from the back of its throat. It forced its head down lower and lower, its jaws snapping inches away from Mia's face, its rancid breath making her eyes water. She felt her arms weakening, her elbows beginning to buckle under the dog's immense weight.

The dog threw itself to one side, twisting its head at the same time, and nipped at Mia's wrist. She cried out as she rolled over with the dog, trying to maintain her grip on it. Its bite hadn't broken the skin, but it still hurt like crazy. The dog kicked out against her, its head thrashing even more violently than before. It managed to break free from Mia's grip and darted just out of reach, its tongue lolling from its mouth as it gasped for breath. It glared at her with malevolent intent, its tail twitching. It crouched down, ready to pounce once more.

Then a blinding blue light filled Mia's vision. Everyone froze, including the dog, as they stared up at it.

The flying saucer dropped like a stone to hover fifteen feet above the ground near the centre of the clearing. Its underside seemed to shimmer for a couple of seconds, then nine Angels fell from it all at once, their elongated arms raised above their heads like they had been squeezed through a narrow tube.

Mia rolled over and scrabbled into the bushes the boy and the dog had sprung from. She stared out at the Angels as they began to spread out away from the ship. It was the first time she had ever seen any close up, and they were a lot taller than she imagined they would be from the newspaper and television reports she had seen of them.

They were almost twelve feet tall, and this close to them she could see their bodies were covered in small scales, like those of a fish. They seemed to be naked, the only thing that could loosely be called clothing a blue disk about six inches in diameter worn on their chests. They had no recognisable sexual organs and all looked identical, as if they had been cast from the same mould. But it was the single eye in the centre of each of their elongated heads that drew most of her attention. Perfectly round black orbs that defied you to look away from them. Unblinking. Mesmerising. Every instinct told Mia to get the hell out of there, but all she could do was continue staring.

Then the dog bared its teeth and barked furiously as it ran at the group of Angels. One of them spun toward it, emitting a series of short, clicking chirps. The dog pounced, its jaws wide and ready to tear the alien apart. But before it could get within range, huge claws sprang from the centre of the Angel's suckers and swiped at the dog in mid-air. The dog yelped as the razor-sharp claws sliced through its flesh. It whimpered pitifully on the ground beside the Angel as its intestines spilled from its body.

The boy roared in anger and thrashed from side to side beneath Suzy. Wicked Tina searched the long grass frantically for the shotgun she had dropped there. The Angels turned as one and plodded slowly toward Suzy and the boy, walking with a jerking movement like vertical stick insects. The boy managed to free himself and ran at the Angels with a scream of anguish and pure hate. Suzy bolted upright and ran away from them and disappeared into the woods. Wicked Tina continued fumbling in the grass for the fallen shotgun.

Mia watched from her hiding place in the bush. It was as if it all happened in slow motion. An Angel reached down and plucked the boy from the ground with one hand. Mia looked away instinctively, not wanting to see the Angel's claws rip his body in half. When his shrill half-bark, half-snarl continued, she looked back up. The Angel had its long fingers curled over the top of the boy's head, its suckers attached to his temples and forehead. It held him at arm's length, as if it were studying him. The boy's legs thrashed wildly, making his body swing to and fro. He reached out for the Angel's eye and tried to gouge it with his fingers, but the Angel held him just out of reach.

"Hey ugly," Wicked Tina shouted.

She'd found the shotgun, and held it at waist-height, the barrel pointing up at the Angels towering above her. She jerked back the trigger. An Angel's eye disintegrated into a yellow and black pulp. The Angel let out a piercing squeal, then spun around flailing its arms, spraying yellow fluid in a wide arc. The other Angels ignored it and continued advancing on Wicked Tina while it continued spinning for a few more seconds, then fell with a loud crash. Wicked Tina backed away, keeping pace with their advance, while she broke open the shotgun, ejected the empty shells, and took spare cartridges from her leather jacket pocket. An Angel reached out for her. She reloaded the shotgun and fired. The Angel flew back and collided with another Angel close behind it, bowling it over. Wicked Tina fired again, and another Angel fell. She ran to a nearby tree, reaching into her pocket for more cartridges as she ran.

An Angel plucked the blue disk from its chest and held it out in one hand, pointing at the tree Wicked Tina hid behind. The disk glowed. Mia felt the hairs on the back of her neck become rigid. She caught a whiff of ozone, then heard a sharp crack as a narrow beam of pure blue light shot from the centre of the disk. Smouldering pieces of bark exploded from the tree shielding Wicked Tina. Flames shot up its trunk like it had been doused in petrol. Leaves crackled and burned, birds fled in terror. Wicked Tina swore, then fired once more before she ran. The Angels plodded after her, then fell down onto all fours and galloped through the woods in pursuit.

Mia looked back at the alien ship. It still hovered fifteen feet above the ground. There was no sign of the boy, or the Angel that held him, they had both vanished. She crept out of the bush, ready to run if any more Angels came out of the ship. In the distance, Wicked Tina's shotgun blasted, but Mia knew there would be nothing she could do to help while she was still unarmed. She circled around the spaceship, keeping her eyes on it the whole time, then ran back to the road and vaulted over the wall. She unfastened a saddle-bag on her bike and took out her shotgun. She cracked it open to make sure both barrels were loaded, then checked her pockets for spare cartridges. She only had six left, so every shot would need to count.

She ran down the road, running parallel to the woodland

on the opposite side of the wall, listening out for any signs of life, hoping she wasn't already too late. Wicked Tina's shotgun blasted somewhere deep in the woods. Mia climbed over the wall and made her way toward the source of the sound. There was another blast, then Wicked Tina's shouted voice.

"Shit! Leg it, quick!"

Wicked Tina and Suzy ran through the trees together, five Angels galloping after them, closing the gap quickly. Wicked Tina turned and threw her shotgun at one of them. It glanced off it, the Angel barely breaking stride. Mia ran to intercept, trying to aim the shotgun as she ran. She barrelled into a tree, panting, and aimed around its trunk, waiting for the Angels to come into range. She fired. An Angel tumbled onto its side and rolled over, yellow fluid spurting from its body. The others continued, ignoring their fallen comrade's plight. Mia fired again at their flank and took down another one. She unzipped a pocket and took out two more cartridges, broke the shotgun open to eject the spent shells, and reloaded it. But the Angels were already out of range by the time she was ready to fire again, so she ran deeper into the woodland after them.

Suzy stumbled and fell. An Angel pounced on her and held her aloft by the waist in one hand, like a prize trophy. Suzy squirmed in its grip and raked her fingernails down its arm, kicking her legs out wildly. The Angel made a series of chirping sounds and reached out with its other hand. Its long fingers curled over the crown of Suzy's head, and once it held her securely it let go of her waist. Suzy's body dangled in its hand as it turned and slowly waddled back toward the spaceship with its kicking and screaming prize.

Mia watched it go, torn between following it or going after the remaining two Angels chasing Wicked Tina. She made a snap decision and followed the plodding Angel with Suzy. She didn't know why it seemed to want her alive, but she knew if it got her into the flying saucer she would be lost forever. Mia darted from tree to tree until she got ahead of the Angel, then crouched down behind a bush and waited for it to appear.

The Angel plodded toward her, with Suzy swinging from its outstretched hand like a Christmas tree bauble. Mia waited until it was almost upon her, then sprang out and swung the shotgun up at its eye. The Angel chirped and reached out for her with its free hand. Mia blasted it with both barrels at close range. Yellow and black matter exploded from the top of the Angel's head and splattered on the ground. The Angel spun as it fell, its hand still clamped around Suzy's head. She cried out as she swung through the air and crashed down alongside it. Mia dropped the shotgun and rushed over to her. She tried to prise the Angel's suckers off Suzy's head, but they were stuck tight, as if they were glued on.

"Get this bloody thing off me!" Suzy yelled. She sat up and struggled to get away from the dead Angel.

"I can't, it won't come off. Hold still, you're making it harder."

Mia took out her knife and hacked at the Angel's wrist. It felt like cutting through a crab's claw. The scaled skin was hard like an external shell, the insides soft and gooey like those of an insect. Viscous yellow pus oozed out and dribbled down the Angel's outstretched arm as she cut through it. It smelled like mouldy fish that had been left out in the sun for too long, and made both women gag. The Angel's arm fell away, the yellow fluid pouring onto the ground, but its long fingers remained firmly clamped around Suzy's head.

Suzy tried to tug one of the fingers free, grimacing in pain as she pulled at it. It tore loose and took a clump of hair with it. Suzy cried out and tossed it away, then reached for another.

"Just leave them," Mia said. "We can cut them off later."

"No, I want them off now!" Suzy yelled, a hint of hysteria in her voice.

"Okay, okay. You hold it up, I'll cut it."

Mia wiped the knife's blade on the grass, then pushed it into Suzy's hair. Suzy grabbed one of the Angel's fingers and stretched it tight. She gritted her teeth while Mia sawed through her hair, then rubbed her sore scalp after the finger came away, huge clumps of hair stuck to its underside. She grabbed the remaining finger, then that too was cut free, leaving behind a bald patch on Suzy's scalp.

Mia picked up the shotgun and reloaded it. "Okay, let's go. There's two of them left, but they seem easy enough to kill. God knows why the army couldn't seem to manage it, the useless bastards." Without waiting for Suzy, she ran back through the woods in the direction she had last seen Wicked Tina.

She found her standing in a drainage ditch, holding the two

Angels at bay with a rotting tree branch. Each time an Angel reached down for her she swung the branch and it recoiled away from her. They were both making high-pitched chirping sounds, as if they were commanding Wicked Tina to put the branch down and come quietly.

Mia crept closer and aimed. She shot one of the Angels in the back and it toppled into the drainage ditch with a high-pitched squeal. The other Angel spun around impossibly fast and plucked the blue disk from its chest. The disk glowed, then cracked as a blue laser beam zipped past Mia's shoulder, missing her by inches. Its intense heat scorched the side of her face, and a bush behind her exploded into flames and was reduced to ashes in a matter of seconds. Mia dived for the ground just before another beam shot from the disk. It whizzed over her and hit a nearby tree.

Wicked Tina climbed out of the drainage ditch and brought the tree branch crashing down on the Angel's outstretched arm. The branch splintered into two. The Angel turned to face her with a series of loud chirps. The blue disk pointed down at her. Wicked Tina swung the remains of the branch at the disk as it began to glow, and knocked the Angel's aim off course. A blue beam tore into the ground nearby and reduced the grass to black ashes. Wicked Tina raised her arm to shield her face from its intense heat.

Mia struggled to her feet and aimed the shotgun, but the Angel was too close to Wicked Tina and she couldn't risk firing in case she hit her, too.

"Get down!" she yelled.

But Wicked Tina had other ideas. She held the branch above her head in both hands, like a huge dagger, and jabbed its splintered end at the Angel's body. The Angel squealed as the wood punctured its hard skin and sank into it. It swiped at Wicked Tina with one hand, its claws extended. Wicked Tina ducked and wrenched the branch free as the Angel's talons whooshed harmlessly over her head. She raised the branch over her shoulder and swung it at one of the alien's legs with a grunt. The leg snapped where she struck it with a sound like a giant shrimp being torn in half. The Angel toppled over sideways and crashed down into the wet grass, where it flailed its arms and thrashed around with ear-piercing squeals. Wicked Tina clubbed its other leg into a sticky mush, keeping well out of the way of the Angel's deadly claws.

Mia walked closer, pointing the shotgun at the prone Angel. She blew off one of its arms at the shoulder, then reloaded and blew off the other. Twigs snapped behind her. Mia turned sharply, but it was just Suzy walking toward her. She turned back to the Angel and looked down at it. She felt no pity as she watched it writhe in agony, and would have quite happily just watched it die slowly if Wicked Tina hadn't rammed the end of the branch into its eye. She stepped back in revulsion as warm sticky fluid splashed over her.

Wicked Tina panted before her, her arms and face covered in yellow goo. She placed a boot on one of the Angel's wrists to hold it down and tried to pull the blue disk from its grip, but it wouldn't budge so she took the dagger from her boot and hacked it off, then held the disk up triumphantly in one hand, the Angel's fingers still curled around it.

"What are you going to do with that?" Mia asked.

"See if I can figure out how to use it."

"Yeah well, watch where you're pointing it when you do. Come on, let's go before more Angels show up to see what's going on. We'll have to leave the bikes where they are and pick them up when it gets dark, in case there's any more of them lurking around here."

12

They found Margot and Fat Brenda's bikes parked at the side of the road leading into town, near a high-rise block of flats with the name Serenity House printed on a plaque above the main entrance door. In front of the tall, grey building was a patch of overgrown grass, with a rusting climbing frame at its centre and a pair of swings made from old lorry tyres.

They hopped over a small, moss-covered wall and ran across the grass to the entrance of the flats. The main door, painted a drab grey in colour that matched the grim look of the building itself, was unlocked, and Mia pushed it open. She had already mentally prepared herself for the stench she would meet inside, but it still made her eyes water as she crossed the threshold. The remains of dozens of bodies littered the concrete floor, little more than gnawed piles of rags and bones after being scavenged by rats and other wildlife. Wicked Tina walked into the gloomy lobby behind her and swore. Suzy covered her mouth and nose with her hands.

"Christ, it makes you appreciate sleeping in bloody car parks and shit, doesn't it?" she said.

"If you think this is bad, wait until you try one of the flats, honey," Wicked Tina replied.

Suzy's face paled as she gaped at her.

A dull thud came from Mia's right. She spun toward it in alarm, expecting to see hordes of Angels lumbering toward her. Grey, graffiti-covered lift doors stood in an alcove nearby, next to stone steps leading up to the first floor. She walked up to the lift doors and listened, sure that was where the sound came from. Something fell down the lift shaft, bumping and scraping off the walls on its descent. It landed six feet below ground level with another dull thud. Suzy had come over to investigate for herself, and Mia cast her a quizzical glance.

Suzy shrugged. "Only one way to find out."

They made their way slowly up the stone steps, peering up

into the gloom as they rounded the first corner before continuing up. Another body lay spread-eagled on the landing, its limbs resting at odd angles. Mia stepped over it and continued up. On the first floor she took out her torch and cast it down a dark corridor. It was obvious from the amount of settled dust on the concrete ground nobody had entered or left those flats for several years. They headed up the stairs, and found the same to be true of the second and third floors.

Approaching the fourth floor, Mia heard muffled voices. She motioned for Suzy and Wicked Tina to keep still while she listened, but couldn't make out any of the words. They crept higher, trying to minimise the sound of their motorcycle boots on the stone steps while they listened to the voices. It wasn't until they reached the sixth floor that Mia realised who they belonged to.

"Margot, Brenda, where are you?" she called out.

Fat Brenda leaned over the balcony two stories further up. "Where the hell have you three been?" she yelled down.

"We got a bit sidetracked, we'll tell you about it when we get up there."

Mia, Wicked Tina and Suzy continued up the stairs in silence, and found Margot and Fat Brenda on the eighth floor. They were carrying a corpse between them across the landing, and threw it into the lift shaft. Fat Brenda wiped sweat from her forehead with the palm of her hand while it tumbled down.

"About time you lot showed up," she said. She wrinkled her nose and peered at Wicked Tina, then took out a torch and shone it in her face. "What the hell's all that gunk you're covered in? It bloody reeks."

Wicked Tina smiled. "It's Angel shit, honey."

"You what?"

"We just killed a load of Angels, didn't we? This is the shit that's inside them." She held up the blue disk with the Angel's fingers attached to it. "Oh yeah, and we got this too."

Fat Brenda's torch moved to illuminate the disk. She frowned and stepped closer to inspect it. "What the hell is it?"

"Some sort of weapon, honey. I reckon I might be able to figure out how to use it to kill Angels with."

"Yeah well, first we need to clear all the stiffs off this level so it won't stink so much. And you need to get that gunk washed off you too, it smells even worse."

Mia cast her torch down the corridor. Five adjacent flats had been broken into, their occupants dumped outside the doors. She shivered involuntarily at their level of decomposition.

"Well go on then," Fat Brenda said. "They won't shift themselves."

Mia sighed and followed Suzy to the nearest corpse. It had been a man, Mia could tell that much from its facial hair, but his grey, withered skin gave no clue as to his age. She put down the shotgun and gripped the man's ankle. He was surprisingly light, being little more than dried skin and bones, and Mia was able to drag him to the lift shaft by herself and kick him over the edge.

After the rest of the corpses were cleared, Mia pushed open the door to one of the flats. Sunlight streamed through tattered lace curtains, dazzling her momentarily until her eyes adjusted to the harsh light. A window was open a couple of inches, and Mia tried to open it wider to dispel the stale musty air inside, but it wouldn't open any further due to a chain connected to the windowsill to stop any would-be suicides from jumping out. She thought about looking for a hacksaw to cut the chain with, but decided not to bother. The smell wasn't as bad as it had been in the foyer, and while unpleasant it wasn't overpowering.

She looked out over the woodland. The elevated position gave her a good view of the entire area. The flying saucer was still there, still hovering fifteen feet above the ground. She wondered how long whatever powered it would last before it crashed down. Maybe they could go back during the night and see if they could find a way inside it. She doubted any of them would be able to fly it, but there might be something in there they could use, maybe some alien weapons that would at least give them a chance when they reached Scotland. And if not they could always smash its instruments so it would never fly again.

The flat was sparsely furnished, with a threadbare carpet and faded, red and yellow striped wallpaper that was starting to uncurl from the nicotine-stained ceiling. A portable television with a wire coat hanger used as an aerial stood on top of a wooden crate, with a single battered armchair facing it. At the opposite side of the room, on top of a rickety-looking wooden table, stood a small Calor Gas stove with an empty saucepan on its single hob. On the floor beneath the table, connected to the stove with a rubber hose, was a large red propane cylinder.

Mia turned the dial on the cooker, listened to the gas hiss for a second, then turned it off and walked through a nearby plywood door into a tiny bathroom and toilet. The bath itself was even smaller than the one Mia had at her old bedsit, barely long enough to sit upright without bending your knees, while the toilet had no seat. But they both looked like sheer luxury compared to what she had become used to. She twisted one of the taps and waited for the water to turn from brown to clear, then ran a bath for herself using several saucepans of boiling water to warm it up. She stripped off and climbed in, used a bar of carbolic soap to scrub away months' worth of grime, then lay down flat with her raised legs resting against the wall until the water went cold.

She dried herself down with a grimy towel, tossed her dirty clothes into the murky water left in the bath so she could wash them later, and walked into the bedroom. She found a clean shirt in the wardrobe and wrapped it around herself, then sat down on the unmade single bed. The bed's springs creaked in protest. She could feel one of them poking up and digging into her arse, so she shuffled to the left to avoid it.

A pile of old magazines lay next to the bed and she picked one up to flick through it. It was about gardening, and she wondered what possible use it would have been to the flat's previous tenant. There wasn't so much as a window box to grow anything in, and there were no signs of houseplants anywhere to be seen. She soon lost interest in the magazine and dropped it back on the pile. She lay down and drew the covers over her naked legs and stared up at the ceiling, wishing Bonehead could be there with her.

She must have dozed off, because the next thing she knew she startled awake. Fat Brenda stood over her, shaking her by the shoulders.

"Wake up. There's Angels outside!"

Mia sat up and rubbed the sleep from her eyes. She cocked her head and listened. The distinctive hum of flying saucers came from outside, what sounded like dozens of them. She hurried over to the window and peered through the lace curtains. The air above the woodland was filled with them, the woodland itself illuminated in harsh blue light. As she watched, hundreds of Angels descended and swarmed across the ground like giant locusts, slicing shrubs and bushes to pieces with their claws. If there were any more people living there with the boy, it wouldn't be long before they were found. The Angels Mia and the others had killed earlier that day were incinerated where they lay with multiple shots from the blue disks. A tree exploded into flames. Then another. And another. Dozens more Angels marched down the main road into town, smashing through doors and forcing their way into shops and houses along the way.

Mia's face paled. "Oh shit. They're looking for *us*, aren't they?" She turned to face Fat Brenda. "What do we do?"

Fat Brenda shrugged and headed for the door. Mia grabbed her shotgun and followed, picking up the spare cartridges she had left next to the Calor Gas stove on the way. Margot, Suzy and Wicked Tina stood in the hallway waiting for her.

"They're coming," Suzy said. "We need to bloody well get out of here while we still can."

Margot shook her head. "It's already too late for that. If we go out there now they'll catch us straight away."

"What else can we do? They're searching all the houses, if we stay here they'll find us."

"Yeah well," Fat Brenda said, "maybe this is our best chance to take some of them with us. They'll need to come up those stairs, we can pick them off as soon as they come round the corner."

Mia showed her the cartridges in her hand. "Are you kidding? This is all I've got left now. Tina hasn't even got a shotgun anymore, and Suzy left hers on her bike. So how long do you think we would last?"

"So what would you suggest?"

Mia frowned. "I don't know."

Fat Brenda turned to Wicked Tina. "You figured out how to use that blue gizmo yet?"

Wicked Tina shook her head. "No, it doesn't make any sense. There's no trigger or button or whatever on it, and no markings or anything."

Fat Brenda nodded. "Well that's that then. We'll just have to make do with what we've got. Unless anyone's got any better ideas?"

"There's a toolbox in my flat," Suzy said. Everyone looked at her. She shrugged. "You know, hammers and screwdrivers and shit. Maybe we could board the main door up, stop them getting in?"

"That wouldn't keep them out for long," Mia said. "I saw them outside, it only takes them a few seconds to get through locked doors."

"Worth a try though," Margot said. "At least it would give us a bit more time to figure something else out. Go and get the toolbox, Suzy."

"What about the roof?" Wicked Tina asked, after Suzy had gone.

"They'd see us from the ships," Fat Brenda said. "Then we wouldn't be able to kill any of them before we got zapped."

Margot nodded. "Yeah, maybe, but it's probably our best option. They're flying pretty low right now, so if we stay away from the edges we might be okay."

Suzy rejoined them with a large metal toolbox. She put it down and opened it up, then took out a hammer and a box of nails.

"Change of plan," Margot said. "We're going up onto the roof instead."

"Good idea," Suzy said, nodding. "You do that, I'll join you after I've nailed the front door shut."

"I'll go with you," Mia said, picking up another hammer. She gave Wicked Tina her shotgun and followed Suzy down the stairs.

They only reached the third floor before the building's main door burst open. Mia leaned over the balcony and looked down. Angels flooded into the lobby and ripped the corpses down there to pieces. One prised open the lift doors and stepped through them, then fell down the shaft with a high-pitched wail. Others followed it, and they too tumbled down. Another, just about to join them, stretched out both arms and grabbed onto the sides of the lift opening. It looked down, then pulled the blue disk from its chest and fired down at the corpses lining the bottom of the shaft, incinerating the fallen Angels along with them. There was a loud whump as the desiccated bodies ignited and a huge ball of fire shot up the lift shaft and engulfed the Angel in the doorway. It squealed and thrashed its arms, then toppled down into the shaft. More and more Angels poured into the building and made their way down the corridor to the ground floor flats. Others found the stairway and dropped onto all fours as they began making their way up them.

Mia and Suzy ran back up the stairs, taking them two at a time. As they rounded the corner leading onto the seventh floor they came face to face with Fat Brenda heading down with her shotgun, a look of grim determination on her face.

"What the hell are you doing?" Mia hissed. "We need to get up onto the roof, quick."

"You can if you want," Fat Brenda said without lowering the shotgun. "Me, I'm heading down."

"Don't be daft, they'll kill you."

"So? We both know they will anyway, sooner or later. At least this way I can take some of them with me."

"Come on FB, we talked about this already. Remember the plan, yeah? Get up to Scotland and cause as much damage as we can. Even if you somehow managed to kill every Angel down there it'd still be pointless. There's millions more of the bastards, they probably wouldn't even notice."

"What, so we hide out on the roof and wait for them to get us, that's your new plan?"

"They might not find us up there. So far, they don't even know we're in here. But that all changes as soon as you start shooting."

"Besides," Suzy said, "you could always shoot them from the roof. The doorway up there will be a lot narrower, so they'd only be able to get through it one by one. It'd be like shooting rats in a drainpipe, you couldn't bloody miss."

Fat Brenda nodded. A wide grin spread across her face as she looked down at her shotgun. "Yeah. Then every shot would count. And when it's empty I can use it to stab the bastards in the eye, send them back down again. Well come on then, what are you waiting for?"

Fat Brenda clumped back up the stairs. Mia clasped a hand on Suzy's shoulder. "Well done," she said, smiling.

Suzy grinned back. "Let's just hope they don't think about looking on the bloody roof."

They soon caught up with Fat Brenda, and continued up to the top floor. From below came the muffled sound of doors being smashed open, the chirp of excited Angels, and furniture being ripped apart. Mia hoped they wouldn't have cause to use any of their blue disks inside the flats, the last thing they needed would be a fire raging up the building to go along with the one in the lift shaft.

Fat Brenda was puffing and panting by the time they reached the top floor, her face bright red from the physical exertion. Mia looked around for a way up to the roof. At the end of the corridor leading to the flats on that level she found an emergency exit door, the glass phial used to secure it already smashed. She pushed it open and looked inside. A metal ladder bolted to the wall led up through an enclosed square space, but it was too dark inside to see how far up it went.

"This way," she called out.

Fat Brenda and Suzy joined her. They sent Fat Brenda up first, and watched her climb about seven feet up the ladder before she stopped. She pushed open a hatch at the top and bright sunlight streamed down as she climbed out.

"We need to take the ladder up with us," Suzy said, "that way they won't be able to follow us up there and shit."

Mia nodded, and crouched down to examine the bolts securing the foot of the ladder to the wall. They were old and rusted, and probably hadn't been touched since the building was first constructed. No chance of loosening them, even if they had thought to bring the toolbox up with them. She listened to the noise coming from downstairs and tried to guess which floor the Angels were currently on. Still far enough away not to be any immediate concern, but if she started hammering at the bolts they might hear it.

She pushed the claw of the hammer between the ladder and the wall, just above one of the restraining bolts, and tugged back on the handle. Plaster cracked and fell, revealing raw brickwork beneath. The bolt gave slightly, and she repositioned the hammer to get a better grip. She jerked the handle back, putting all her weight behind it. The bolt's housing came loose with a loud grating sound. Suzy was already working on the other bolt, and soon had that one free too.

Mia put down the hammer and gripped the bottom rung of the ladder in both hands. She tugged it, and heard bolts further up straining and groaning. Suzy climbed up the ladder and went to work on them with her hammer. Plaster and brick dust rained down on Mia and she had to look away to avoid getting it in her eyes. Eventually the ladder came loose from the wall and Suzy cried out when she almost lost her balance. Mia held the ladder steady while Suzy climbed the rest of the way up it and stepped out onto the roof. After following her up, Mia pulled the ladder onto the roof and lay it down next to the hatch. Suzy closed the hatch and nailed it shut to slow down anything trying to follow them up there.

Wicked Tina, Margot and Fat Brenda sat near the centre of the roof, leaning against the large, square chimney that jutted up into the sky. Mia and Suzy joined them and waited. All any of them could do was hope the Angels wouldn't think of looking up there while they listened to them scurrying around in the rooms below.

PART 3

THE SURVIVORS

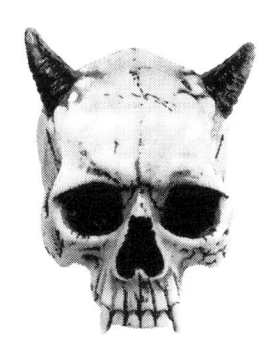

13

Mia didn't have a care in the world. It was a perfect summer day, not a cloud in the sky, the only wind the one blowing in her face. The sun was high, and so was Mia. Not with drugs, that would come later, but with her own endorphins. The Norton Commando vibrated between her legs, adding to the euphoria as she tore down the empty country road with the rest of Satan's Bastards, every one of them aiming for the ton on the straights, then slowing just enough to bank over hard for the bends before accelerating out of them. Bonehead rode beside her, and kept glancing at her and smiling as if he knew something she didn't. Mia tuned him out and concentrated on the road ahead as it whizzed by beneath her feet.

They rode in formation, Dirk at the head, flanked by Tanner and Stevo close behind. Then came Basher and Mike, Skitter and Baz, Andy and Bulldog, followed by the rest of the men riding two or three abreast, taking up the full width of the road. Fat Brenda and Margot led the women, as was their right as old ladies, with Skinny Brenda, Suzy, Wicked Tina, Juicy Lucy and the other mamas at the rear of the pack. Mia knew Bonehead would get a ribbing from the other men for riding with the mamas, and for that she couldn't help loving him a little bit more.

They approached a lay-by with a hotdog van surrounded by dozens of bikers who all turned to wave as they roared past. Mia waved back, feeling like she was the centre of their attention. She glanced in her mirror and saw several men rush to their bikes in order to join the long convoy.

The road twisted and turned through the countryside with a certain familiarity Mia couldn't quite place. She had the feeling she had ridden that road once before, but couldn't remember where it led to. Not that it mattered. It was the journey that counted, not the destination. That was just somewhere to stretch your legs and have a bit of fun with the locals before you hit the road again.

Dirk stretched out his arm and pointed left on the run up to a crossroads. Mia jabbed her rear brake and kicked down the gears as she followed the other bikers onto a road leading into a small village. As always when there was the possibility of innocent children in the road they slowed to a crawl while they rode through the village itself. Citizens going about their daily business stopped and stared. Young children pointed. Dogs barked. Somewhere in the distance, a church bell rang.

Dirk signalled right and the procession of motorcycles turned into a side street. A moment later they pulled up outside a church and revved their engines while they waited for everyone to arrive. Fat Brenda and Margot parked their bikes by the gates and entered a small graveyard at the side of the church. They returned clutching bunches of flowers stolen from the graves, and stood either side of the gates. They smiled at Mia as she parked her bike and climbed off. Bonehead parked beside her and took hold of her hand. Mia looked at him and frowned.

"What's going on?" she asked. "We going to rob a church or something?"

Bonehead grinned at her. "I'm claiming you as me old lady. Why else would you be dressed like that?"

"What?"

Mia looked down at her clothes in surprise. Instead of her usual black leather biker jacket and faded denim jeans she wore a flowing white dress. She lifted it up at the front to inspect her motorcycle boots. They were white too, and were adorned with blue skulls on the buckles. She looked back up at Bonehead and noticed the lace veil hanging down from the front of her motorcycle helmet for the first time.

"For real?" she said, grinning. Her heart felt like it would burst with happiness.

Dirk took Mia by the arm and escorted her to the church, past a row of cheering bikers throwing confetti. Someone was playing her favourite Hawkwind song on the church organ, and she couldn't help humming along with it. Tanner and Basher held the church doors open and she stepped inside with Dirk. Bonehead was already there somehow, even though she hadn't seen him pass her by. He stood by the altar wearing a top hat and a long leather trenchcoat. A catholic priest wearing black robes with an upside-down cross around his neck stood before him, hands spread in welcome. In one hand he held a Haynes Workshop Manual for a Triumph Bonneville 650. In the other was a tattoo gun, ready to make their union permanent with Bonehead's mark of ownership beneath both nipples of Mia's breasts.

Mia took up her place beside Bonehead. He turned to her and smiled. Mia smiled back. She couldn't believe this was happening. She'd always known she was Bonehead's favourite screw from the way he always chose her out of all the other mamas. His sex was gentle, loving, nothing like the animalistic rutting of the other bikers she had been with.

"You know you're all going to die, right?" Bonehead said.

Flames erupted from nowhere and engulfed his entire body. His eyes sizzled and popped. The flesh blackened and melted from his face.

Mia screamed and bolted upright in a cold sweat. She held her head in her hands and sobbed.

Mia, Fat Brenda, Suzy, Margot and Wicked Tina had been living in Serenity House for six days now. It had been over five hours before the Angels moved on further into the town and they were able to come down from the roof to find every flat in the building ransacked. The blue disk Wicked Tina had taken from the Angel in the woods was missing, presumed taken during the search. They retrieved their belongings from the eighth floor and moved into flats on the top floor, so they could be closer to the emergency roof exit in case the Angels came back.

At dusk the Angels retreated to their ships, but instead of leaving they remained hovering over what was left of the nearby woodlands. The following day they were out in force again, spreading out in all directions as they widened their search.

Food and drink had been easy enough to scavenge from the other flats, but everyone was becoming more and more restless with their enforced captivity as the days stretched on with no sign of the Angels giving up. Fat Brenda took it particularly bad, her need for revenge so strong she wanted to take to the streets and blow away as many Angels as she could, but Mia and Margot had always managed to talk her out of it.

Mia wiped the tears and snot from her face with the bedcovers. Suzy was right, there was no point dwelling on the past when it couldn't be changed. If there was an afterlife she would meet up again with Bonehead and the others in Biker Heaven soon enough. And if there wasn't, she wouldn't know any difference anyway so it wouldn't really matter. She shook her head and sighed. She needed to get out of this prison and back on the road where she belonged. Back on her bike, where just navigating the roads would be enough to take her mind off everything else.

Mia slipped on a T-shirt and jeans, then walked over to the bedroom window and looked out. At first she thought the window had misted up, but as she wiped it with her hand she realised it was a low hanging fog she saw, everything outside the window shrouded in a hazy grey mist. She opened the window to the full extent the chain would allow and listened. Birds twittered somewhere close by, but she couldn't hear anything else. No Angel ships humming, no sounds of destruction coming from the nearby town. She rushed out of the door in her bare feet, then barged into Fat Brenda's flat next door. She ran over to the bed Fat Brenda's naked body lay sprawled over and shook her awake.

"I think they've gone!"

"What?" Fat Brenda blinked and rubbed her eyes with her fists.

"The Angels. I think they've finally gone."

Fat Brenda bolted upright and hurried over to the window to see for herself. "Are you sure? I can't see a thing out there."

"Yeah, but listen."

Fat Brenda opened the window and put her ear to the gap. "Can't hear nothing?"

"That's what I mean. There's no humming or anything. And the birds are back."

Fat Brenda nodded. "Get the others up, we'll go and have a look outside." She picked up her clothes from the floor and struggled into them, then joined Mia in the hallway to help rouse the others. Wicked Tina was the hardest to wake, having downed a full bottle of vodka she'd found the night before. Fat Brenda had to slap her face twice before she finally opened her eyes.

"Get dressed, we're going outside."

Wicked Tina groaned, then clasped her head with both hands. "What the hell time is it?"

"How the hell should I know?" Fat Brenda said. "Just get your shit together and meet us downstairs. And don't take too long about it."

Mia returned to her own flat and pulled on her motorcycle boots and leather jacket. She opened a can of chicken soup and drank it cold, then picked up her shotgun and gathered up Suzy and Wicked Tina before making her way downstairs to the foyer. Fat Brenda and Margot were outside, checking their bikes over in the dim light filtering through the fog.

"You see anything?" Mia asked. Fat Brenda shook her head. "I'll have a walk up the hill, see if I can get above the mist."

"I'll go with you," Suzy said. "Might as well fetch our bikes and shit while we're at it."

Wicked Tina nodded. "Yeah."

The three women walked up the hill together, listening out for any sign of Angel activity, and found their motorcycles where they had left them. The mist was just as thick as it had been outside the flats, but Mia was sure if there were any Angels nearby they would have come across them by now. She stuffed the shotgun inside her leather jacket and climbed on her bike, then pulled out the choke and kicked down on the starter. The bike spluttered, but wouldn't start. She tried again, twisting the throttle slightly at the same time. It still wouldn't start. She tried a third time, then a fourth, cursing Suzy and Wicked Tina silently when their bikes rumbled into life behind her. She raised herself up in the saddle and tried putting more weight behind the kick, but that didn't work either.

"You want a push, honey?" Wicked Tina asked. She walked her bike forward until she was level with Mia.

"No, I can manage."

Mia climbed off and pushed the bike to the apex of the hill, picking up speed as she went, then dived onto it and stamped down on the gear lever, twisting the throttle at the same time. The back wheel skidded for a second before it gained traction on the road's surface. The engine whined with a dull growl, then roared into life with a bang and a thick black cloud of smoke belched from the exhaust. The engine backfired a couple more times as she made her way down the hill, back to the flats.

Margot and Fat Brenda were sat on their bikes, looking over their shoulders as Mia approached. She pulled up beside Margot and revved her engine to keep it running.

"What were you shooting at?" Margot asked, peering up the hill as Suzy and Wicked Tina rode down it.

"Nothing," Mia said. "It was just my bike backfiring, that's all."

"No Angels?"

"None at all. Looks like they've all pissed off somewhere else."

"Good," Fat Brenda said. "We should get going too."

"Shouldn't we wait until it gets dark?" Mia asked.

"No point," Margot said. "This fog should hide us well enough. If it starts to thin out we'll find somewhere to stay, but until then we should be okay."

Mia nodded and backed her bike up to make way for Fat Brenda and Margot to pull forward. Wicked Tina and Suzy rode past and followed them down the road. Mia stared at the thick mist swirling around her and sighed. It looked like it was going to be a slow, boring ride, but at least it was better than being cooped up inside.

14

Something about the twisting B road surrounded by open countryside Mia rode down reminded her of a school trip to the Yorkshire Dales when she was thirteen. The bus drove down a road just like this one; she could remember everyone's exaggerated lurches to one side on each bend the bus took, the laughter when Miss Bloom stood up to tell them to settle down, then fell into Mr Stegington's lap when the bus rounded another sharp corner.

They stayed for a week in a youth hostel, little more than a series of large wooden shacks with rickety bunk beds to sleep in. They were supposed to be mapping out the local area in groups of three or four, marking the location of any interesting plants or wild animals they came across. But to Mia it was a stupid and pointless thing to do, especially since the gift shop next to the youth hostel sold maps that detailed every area of interest you could imagine.

So Mia and the other kids from the foster home just wandered through the woods smoking and looking for something more interesting to do. When Mr Steggington asked to see what progress they had made on their map, they told him they weren't ready to show him just yet. The next day, Mia's best friend Carol stole one of the maps from the gift shop and they took turns to copy all the landmarks and places of interest from it.

Mia smiled to herself at the memory, brought on by the fresh scent of open countryside after so much time spent in the rotting towns and cities. It was early evening, they had been riding for about an hour since their last stop at a deserted farm house to pick up fresh shotguns and cartridges. Mia had the lead, with Wicked Tina close behind and the others trailing after them in single file with Suzy taking up the rear. The road twisted and turned, passed over a roaring river, and headed further into the countryside. Mia rode on auto-pilot, her mind full of childhood memories.

On the Friday evening of the school trip, the night before they were due to head back to Retford, a disco was held in the youth hostel's dining hut. Tables and chairs were piled up around the sides of the ramshackle building, with multicoloured flashing Christmas lights strung over them. A glitter ball hung from the rafters and rotated slowly, sending tiny reflections of light swirling over the children dancing beneath it. Mr Stegington stood behind a record player at one side of the hut, and played a selection of Dave Clark Five, Elvis Presley and Beatles songs, interspersed with more modern hits by bands Mia had long since forgotten the names of.

One of the boys had found a bottle of gin hidden under Miss Bloom's mattress, and tipped its contents into the bowl of fruit punch when nobody was looking. Mia had already downed several glasses before anyone told her, and she didn't know why her legs had gone so wobbly. When she found out the punch had been spiked she drank several more glasses, and later in the night she staggered out of the hut arm in arm with the boy responsible.

It was the night she lost her virginity, and even though it was all over within seconds of taking her knickers off and hitching up her skirt she could still remember every detail as if it were yesterday. She tried to remember the boy's name, but came up blank. It was only the act itself she remembered, sprawled out on damp grass with her legs in the air, the world spinning around her, the boy's pimply face gurning down at her when he came. After he pulled his jeans back up Mia rolled over and spewed her guts up. By the time she wiped his spunk off her legs and put her knickers back on the boy was gone. At school on the following Monday, Mia had never been so popular with boys. They flocked around her, all wanting to go on a date, and—

"Mia, look out!"

The warning shout came from Wicked Tina and shocked Mia back to the present. Her eyes bulged and her mouth dropped open when she caught a glimpse of something stretched across the road before her. A thin rope four feet from the ground, tied between two adjacent trees. Rear wheels skidded on the dusty road as the others slammed on the brakes, but Mia knew it was already too late for her as she sped toward it.

She raised her arms to protect her face, and the taut rope struck her wrists like a sledgehammer and flung her backwards while her bike continued forward under its own momentum. Instinct took over and she raised her knees and twisted her body so she could roll on impact like Basher had taught her so many times. But then the buckle of her left boot caught on one of the straps securing her sleeping bag to the back of her bike and snapped her leg straight. Her arms flailed in the air as her body swung down head-first and the tarmac rushed toward her. Then the bike toppled sideways, sending her spinning through the air like a rag doll.

Her boot tore itself free as she spun, and she just had enough time to clutch the top of her head and cover her face with her arms before she slammed down shoulder-first and rolled over and over the tarmac into the hedgerow by the side of the road. She came to a rest face-down in long, damp grass and lay there for several seconds before she dared to move. She could taste blood in her mouth. Her knees ached with a dull throbbing pain. She reached down and probed one of them gingerly, and felt pieces of grit and torn denim in the open wound. Her hand came away bloody. She wiped it on the grass and rolled onto her back, wondering why none of the other women had gone to her aid yet. Had they managed to stop in time, or were they in a similar position themselves, lying injured at the side of the road? She sat up and took off her helmet and goggles. She'd better go and find out where they were.

Then she saw the man staring down at her.

A man in filthy army fatigues, a crooked grin on his grime-covered face.

Holding a pistol, with its barrel pointed directly at Mia's face.

"Who the hell are you, and what do you want?" she asked.

"Shut it," the man growled in a broad Glaswegian accent. He had shoulder-length matted ginger hair, and looked to be in his mid- to late-twenties. "Face down lassie, hands behind your back."

Mia wondered how fast his reflexes would be, if she could spring up and grab the gun off him before he had time to react. If he wanted her dead he would have already shot her by now, so he must want her alive for something, just like the Angels had back at the woods. Mia could use that to her advantage. If he hesitated before shooting, that might just give her the split second she needed to overpower him.

"I wouldn't do that if I were you," the man said, as if he could read Mia's mind. He stepped back out of her reach, the pistol still trained on her. "One less lassie won't make any real difference, so don't go thinking you're anything special here because you're not. Now lie back down on your stomach and put your hands behind your back, or I'll blow your pretty little head off."

Mia lay down and rolled onto her stomach as commanded, her head turned to one side so she could keep an eye on the man with the gun. He walked toward her slowly, the pistol still aimed at her head. Mia waited for her chance, her muscles tensed and ready to spring. He took another step closer.

Then another.

Mia quickly rolled onto her side, grabbed the ankle of his boot mid-step with one hand, and yanked on it. He cried out in surprise, but somehow managed to keep his balance on one leg. He hopped closer, struggling against Mia's grip, then launched himself at her with one elbow raised. Mia released his ankle and tried to roll out of the way, but she wasn't quick enough. The man flopped down on her, his elbow digging into her stomach like a lance, and the air whooshed out of her lungs with a gasp. The man flipped her over and squatted down on the small of her back.

"Stupid wee bitch," he said, grabbing her left hand. "You're going to regret that."

He wrenched Mia's arm up her back with a savage jerk. Mia sucked in a lungful of air and cried out in agony. The man shuffled himself up her back and held her arm in place with his knee, then took hold of her right arm and pulled her hands together. He looped something around her wrists and pulled it tight. Whatever it was it was hard, thin, and dug into her flesh when she tried to pull her hands apart. The weight lifted from her back and Mia was hauled to her feet by her armpits and pushed forward.

Suzy and Fat Brenda were on their knees in the centre of the road, looking down at the tarmac, their hands fastened behind their backs with thin plastic cable-ties. Two men wearing camouflage clothing stood behind them with rifles pointed at the back of their heads. Mia's captor pushed her toward them with a shove to the back. One of the two men turned and aimed his rifle at her while the other searched her pockets. He pulled out Mia's knife and tossed it into the hedgerow, then patted her down and ordered her to kneel beside Fat Brenda.

When Mia didn't comply he grabbed her hair and kicked out at the back of her legs. She crashed down, her already lacerated knees taking the brunt of the impact against the hard tarmac. She cried out and lurched forward. He held her upright by her hair and placed the barrel of his gun against the back of her head. Mia gritted her teeth, determined not to give him the satisfaction of hearing her cry out once more. Tears of pain rolled down her cheeks.

Further down the road, Wicked Tina and Margot crouched behind their bikes, shotguns trained on the three men behind Mia, Fat Brenda and Suzy. Mia knew there was little they could do to help them. If they fired at the three men, the scattershot of the shotgun cartridges might take out the women too. But the stalemate gave her a small glimmer of hope. Maybe they would aim high, and distract the men long enough for Fat Brenda and Suzy to do something. Mia knew she was in no fit state to help them fight, but if she flung herself back she might still be able to unbalance the man holding her. Then it would be up to Fat Brenda and Suzy to finish him off.

"I'd put those guns down if I were you, ladies," a male voice said from somewhere to Mia's right. "It'd be a shame to kill you after we've gone to all this trouble."

He stepped into view holding a submachine gun in both hands. He was older than the others, late-thirties Mia guessed, bald-headed, and had a bushy brown beard with a few grey hairs in it. Without giving any further warning, he spun the submachine gun to point at Wicked Tina and a short burst of staccato shots rang out.

"No!" Mia yelled.

Wicked Tina dived to one side, but the bullets tore into her bike's saddle-bag instead. The bag split open and canned food and drinks rolled across the road. A whisky bottle shattered and spilled its contents.

"Perhaps you didn't hear me, ladies," the man with the submachine gun said calmly. "I said, I'd put those guns down if I were you. Next time you won't be so lucky."

Mia noticed four more men scattered around the woodland by the side of the road. Three held pistols, while the other had a rifle with a sniper sight. The one with the rifle stood with his legs apart, aiming at Margot, while the others spread out to cover Wicked Tina from all angles.

Margot tossed her shotgun over the bike she crouched behind and stood up with her hands raised. Wicked Tina swore at her, then raised up herself and aimed at the man with the submachine gun.

"You shoot me and it'll be the last thing you ever do, you ugly bastard."

The man laughed. "Slack, Garratt, Davis. If she hasn't put her Farmer Giles pop-gun down within the next five seconds, shoot those women."

"Yes, Sergeant Harper," the three men behind Mia shouted in unison.

Wicked Tina's head snapped toward them. "No!" she shouted. Her hands shook and her shotgun wavered.

One of the men with the pistols rushed forward, head bowed, and barrelled into her, head-butting her in the stomach. Wicked Tina lost her balance and flew backwards. She landed heavily on her arse and flopped down onto her back with the man on top of her. He grabbed the shotgun and wrenched it out of her hand, then tossed it far into the bushes behind her. Wicked Tina screamed at him and raked at his face with her fingernails. He raised a fist and punched her twice in the forehead, knocking her out cold. Two of the other men grabbed Margot and forced her to her knees, then secured her hands behind her back with a cable-tie.

The man with the submachine gun, Sergeant Harper, strode over to Mia with a leering grin on his face. "Now then," he said, standing before her, "just where the hell did you all think you were going to in such a hurry?"

"To finish your job for you, you filthy cowards," Fat Brenda shouted, glaring up at the man.

Harper turned to face her. "Oh? And what job would that be then?"

"We're going to kill the Angels, something you bastards should have done five years ago."

Harper laughed. "I see," he said. "How very noble of you, I'm sure. And just how were you planning to do that? No, never mind, I don't really care."

"You've made a big mistake here," Mia said. "Our friends aren't far behind, and when they get here they'll kill you all. So the best thing you can do right now is let us go and slink off back to wherever it is you came from. Maybe you'll be lucky and we won't tell them what's happened here."

Harper laughed again. "We both know that's not going to happen. We've been watching you ever since you left that farm, and we know you're alone." He turned to each of the motorcycles in turn and shredded their back tyres with short blasts from the submachine gun. "Get them in the truck," he said.

"Yes, Sergeant Harper."

Mia screamed as she was dragged to her feet by her hair. Her legs wobbled and her knees threatened to give way beneath her. Suzy was on her feet too, bent almost double by the man holding her by her bound wrists. Fat Brenda remained kneeling, refusing to budge while her captor struggled to lift her. He eventually gave up and threatened to shoot her instead. Fat Benda sneered at him while she rose up slowly in defiance, and got a backhander across the face in return.

Two men picked up Wicked Tina by her wrists and ankles and carried her toward them. She came round and writhed and squirmed in their grip, shouting obscenities at them. She managed to twist one hand free, then dug her fingernails into the wrist of the man holding her other hand. He cried out and dropped her. Wicked Tina twisted as she fell, and managed to stop her head from cracking down against the tarmac by landing on her shoulder. She kicked out at the man holding her ankles, but he held her tight. He twisted her onto her back, then raised her legs high above her head and leaned his weight against them, pinning Wicked Tina's shoulders against the ground like a professional wrestler performing a finishing move. Wicked Tina screamed at him to let her go, but he just laughed.

"Anderson, get hold of her arms," he shouted.

The other man, Anderson, bent down and tried to grab Wicked Tina's thrashing arms. She spat up at him and tried to claw at his eyes. He snatched one of her wrists and wrenched her arm down, then held it in place with his boot while he tried to get hold of her other hand. Wicked Tina landed a wild punch to the side of his head. He cried out. She swung her fist back for another blow, but Anderson saw this one coming and he was ready for it. He blocked it with the palm of his hand, then closed his fist around hers and twisted her arm savagely. Wicked Tina cried out in pain. She struggled and bucked her hips, but couldn't free herself from the two men's grip.

"About bloody time, you pair of useless bastards," Sergeant Harper said. "Now get her on her feet and get her trussed up. If she pulls anything like that again just shoot the bitch."

Anderson stretched out Wicked Tina's arms while the other man twisted her legs to flip her over onto her stomach. As her body turned, Anderson stepped over her and pulled her hands together. He held her wrists in one hand while he reached into his combat jacket for a cable-tie, then looped it over her wrists and pulled it tight. The man holding her ankles released her and darted forward to help Anderson haul her to her feet. She continued to struggle in their grip.

"Get off me, you ugly bastards!"

Anderson smiled. "Ooh, a feisty one. I think I'll have this one for myself."

"The hell you will," the other man said. "We agreed, no dibs on any of them."

"Pack it in, you two," Sergeant Harper said. "Any more arguments and you both get the fat one. Now get going, you've wasted enough of our time as it is."

Mia's captor tightened his grip around her hair and spun her around to face the opposite direction. She gritted her teeth and tried not to cry out as he forced her to march, head bowed, down the road before him. Wicked Tina, somewhere close behind, kept up her tirade of abuse. Fat Brenda screamed in rage. But Mia, Margot and Suzy remained silent, resigned to their fate.

15

The soldiers marched them round a sharp left-hand bend half a mile away, where they came to two armoured vehicles blocking the road. They looked old and battered, the dark green camouflage paintwork scorched down to bare metal in places, their undercarriages and huge, off-road tyres caked in dried mud. One of the vehicles, a squat rectangular jeep, had a machinegun turret mounted on it, accessed through a hatch in the roof. A bearded man in camouflage clothing stood there, holding the machinegun in both hands as he watched the group approach. Another man sat in the driver's seat, and tossed a cigarette out of the side window. He stepped out of the jeep and saluted at Sergeant Harper, then ran to the back of the other vehicle, a six-wheeled personnel carrier, and opened up its rear doors.

The women were taken over to the personnel carrier and ordered inside at gunpoint. With their hands still bound behind their backs they had to worm their way inside on their stomachs, wriggling themselves across the floor of the vehicle while the watching men laughed at their antics. The men climbed in after them and took up seats on wooden benches lining both sides of the truck, while the women lay sprawled between them on the cold metal floor. Wicked Tina tried to kick out at the ankles of those sitting closest to her. One of them raised the butt of his rifle and slammed it down on the side of her head, knocking her unconscious once more. The rear doors slammed shut, and seconds later the engine rumbled into life with a deafening roar and the truck lurched forward. Mia felt the bare metal floor vibrate beneath her as it picked up speed. They were all thrown from side to side as it took sharp bends without slowing.

Fifteen minutes later the vehicle came to a stop. By then Wicked Tina had regained consciousness, and moaned softly to herself. Blood trickled from a small cut above one eye, surrounded by an angry red welt where she had been struck by the rifle butt. The rear doors opened and the men climbed out in formation, jumping down in pairs onto loose gravel. They lined up facing the rear of the truck and aimed their pistols and rifles inside.

"Out!" Anderson ordered, stepping forward. He holstered his pistol and stood to one side of the doors.

Fat Brenda, who was in front of Mia, rolled herself to the edge of the truck and planted her feet on the ground. Anderson grabbed her by the arm and hauled her upright, then shoved her to one side and beckoned Mia forward. Mia shuffled herself to the rear of the vehicle. As soon as she was within reach Anderson dragged her the rest of the way and pulled her upright. She joined Fat Brenda by the side of the truck and looked around, trying to ignore all the rifles pointed at her, while Margot, Suzy and Wicked Tina were unloaded from the truck.

They were in a car park attached to a small visitor centre with seven wooden huts nearby, a similar layout to the one Mia had stayed at during her school trip all those years ago. At the far end of the car park, taking up four parking spaces, stood an Esso petrol tanker. As Mia watched, three men in dirty camouflage clothing stepped out of one of the huts. One wolf-whistled and made obscene gestures at Wicked Tina. Another laughed and jeered at Fat Brenda. Sergeant Harper ordered them all back inside with a curt shout, and they complied immediately.

The women were marched at gunpoint toward the gift shop. The first thing that struck Mia as she walked through the door was the electricity still worked — the building was lit by fluorescent strip lighting that hummed gently, and she could hear bland music playing quietly through wall-mounted speakers. All the shelves and merchandise had been removed from the building; in their place stood neat rows of canned food and bottled drinks on wooden pallets.

Anderson opened a door marked Staff Only behind the till counter and the women were ushered inside. A single lightbulb hung from the ceiling and cast a dim orange glow over the room. It looked like a small staff canteen, with a sink and worktop at one end, but all the other furniture had been removed. There were no windows, no other way out. The door slammed behind them and locked, the key removed. The soldiers murmured to each other and laughed as they left the gift shop.

"What do you think they want with us?" Suzy asked quietly.

"Use your imagination, honey," Wicked Tina said. "What the hell do you think they want us for? What have men always wanted women for?"

Fat Brenda sneered. "Yeah well, if any of them come near me they'll get more than they bargained for, I'll tell you that now."

"So what do we do?" Mia asked.

"We wait until someone opens that door again, then we kill them," Fat Brenda said.

"What, with our hands tied behind our backs? What are we going to do, bite them to death?"

Wicked Tina smiled. "The dumb bastards didn't think to search me properly," she said. "I've still got my dagger in my boot. Only thing is, I can't reach it with my hands tied up like this so one of you will need to get it out for me."

"I'll do it," Suzy said.

She lay down at Wicked Tina's feet, with her back to her. Wicked Tina knelt on the ground and Suzy's bound hands fumbled blindly with the hem of her jeans to raise it above the motorcycle boot she kept her dagger in. Mia caught a glimpse of its ivory handle and spoke words of encouragement. Suzy's face screwed up in concentration as she struggled to grip it with her fingertips.

"Got it," she said eventually.

Wicked Tina shuffled herself back along the floor and the dagger slid out of her boot. Suzy rolled onto her stomach, holding its serrated blade pointing up, the handle clasped between her hands. Mia straddled her and knelt down, facing her feet. With verbal instructions from Wicked Tina, she positioned her hands either side of the blade and jerked back and down against it. The plastic strap around her wrists snapped with an audible twang. Her wrists were red where it had dug into them, and she rubbed them before taking the dagger from Suzy and cutting her free. Suzy took the dagger and freed the others, then gave it back to Wicked Tina.

Then they all stood by the door and waited for one of the soldiers to come back so they could overpower him and gain their freedom.

They waited.

And waited.

An hour later they were still waiting.

Suzy paced the small room, occasionally gazing at the locked door and sighing. Wicked Tina sat on the worktop and tossed her dagger from hand to hand. Fat Brenda slumped down with her back to the door and stared into space. Margot kept crouching down to peer through the keyhole, then shaking her head.

Mia sat against the far wall and picked bloody grit and threads of denim from her knees. With nothing else to do while she waited for one of the soldiers to return for them, her mind wandered back to that day in Rotherham she had thought would be her last one on earth.

Flying saucers filled the sky. Dozens and dozens of them, zipping by overhead in all directions. RAF fighter jets shot at them, but their missiles just seemed to explode in the air and caused no damage to the ships themselves. Blue lasers fired back and fighter jets exploded into balls of flame before tumbling down in pieces.

Mia tore down the road on her Norton Commando, Bonehead keeping pace with her on his Honda 650, chasing after the rest of Satan's Bastards as they sped away from the chaos all around them. The driver of the grey Ford Cortina who had knocked Bonehead off his bike stood beside his wrecked car and stared up at the sky with his mouth hanging open. Mia and Bonehead ignored him as they weaved around him.

Back on the straight road, Mia twisted the throttle and gained some ground on the others. Bonehead kept pace with her and rode alongside on her right. A sharp left hand bend came up fast. The other bikers took the bend wide and banked over hard with their foot-pegs almost touching the ground. Mia let Bonehead pull ahead and followed their lead, drifting over to the left before she reached the bend, then using the full width of the road to straighten out the curve. It was a big risk, if anything was coming from the opposite direction she wouldn't see it in time to avoid it, but she had no time to think about that. If she didn't get out of there soon she would join the other burnt corpses by the roadside.

Another RAF plane exploded overhead and burning

shrapnel plummeted to the ground half a mile to Mia's right. On her left, black smoke billowed into the sky as a farm building blazed out of control. Then, from the swirling smoke, came an Angel ship flying low, barely twenty feet from the ground. It shot toward her at a phenomenal speed, and closed in on her within a matter of seconds. She shouted a warning to Bonehead, who had fallen back into formation with her. Bonehead looked for himself, then swore. Both bikes accelerated up to eighty in an attempt to out-run it.

The Angel saucer kept pace with them, flying less than six yards behind. Its regular hum increased in pitch and volume, then a blue laser shot out from the centre of its underside. Mia felt the shockwave as it flew past her and hit a tree by the side of the road. She grabbed her front brake and stamped down hard on the rear. Bonehead followed her lead a couple of seconds later and the Angel ship thundered past overhead.

Bonehead dabbed his bike back until he was level with Mia again. Mia looked at him wide-eyed, and saw her own fear reflected in his face. They watched the saucer close in on one of the other bikers and shouted out a warning, but the bike was too far away for its rider to hear them. Another laser shot down and the motorcycle exploded, sending shrapnel and bloody clumps of its rider flying in all directions. A metal shard from the bike's petrol tank struck one of the other riders on the side of the head and he went down, his motorcycle tumbling end over end as he fell from it.

Mia rode forward to help, weaving around bits of burning motorcycle littering her path, but it was obvious when she got there the rider was dead. His arms and legs and half his face were missing, his skull cracked open and seeping grey matter. It looked like Stevo from the build of the torso, but she couldn't be sure. It could've been anyone, it was impossible to tell from what was left of him. Bonehead pulled up beside her and swore when he looked down at the body.

The flying saucer continued on its path of destruction. Another bike exploded. Others slammed on their brakes and let the ship pass them by, then turned around and sped back the way they had come. Only four bikes remained in front of the ship. One tried to escape offroad into the surrounding countryside, but the bike's front wheel caught in a drainage ditch by the side of the road and catapulted its rider over the handlebars. Bonehead twisted his throttle and shot forward. Mia swore, then followed him up the road. Bikes tore past her in the opposite direction. Fat Brenda flashed her headlight in warning and yelled something.

Bonehead climbed off his bike and ran to the fallen biker. It was Basher, and he'd been lucky enough to land on something soft. Bonehead pulled him to his feet, then helped him limp back to the road. Mia watched on while they strained together to right Basher's motorcycle and pull it out of the ditch. Another motorcycle exploded in the distance. Bonehead, Basher and Mia all looked at the same time.

Then the flying saucer spun in a short arc and headed back toward them.

"Leave it!" Mia shouted, turning her bike around. "Get the hell out of there, quick!"

Bonehead and Basher dropped the motorcycle in the ditch and ran to Bonehead's bike. Basher waited while he did a U-turn, then dived on the back.

Mia twisted the throttle and let the clutch out quickly. Her bike surged forward, its front wheel raising from the ground with the sudden harsh acceleration. She leaned forward over the petrol tank to get it back down, and kicked up through the gears as she sped down the road.

To Mia's left, three more RAF jet fighter planes roared over the horizon to join the battle in the sky. One broke away and headed in her direction. It flew in a wide arc over the field and launched two missiles at the Angel ship in pursuit of the bikers. The missiles exploded harmlessly inches away from the ship. The plane roared overhead, banking over to turn for another strike. The Angel ship zipped into the air at a bone-crushing speed and flew to intercept the plane as it began to make another approach.

Mia and Bonehead rode on, desperate to get away as the plane exploded behind them. Half a mile further down the road, Wicked Tina stood beside her bike and waved them down. More explosions came from the sky as they pulled up beside her. In the distance a plane spiralled down with a discordant whine, one of its wings missing, its fuselage on fire.

"What's up?" Mia asked.

"I came back to let you know where we're going," Wicked

Tina said, climbing on her bike. "There's some sort of nature reserve about thirty miles that way, we saw it mentioned on a road sign. We're going to hide out there until the army or whoever sorts all this shit out."

Mia nodded grimly, while Bonehead set off down the road with Basher clinging to his chest. Wicked Tina kick-started her bike and followed them. Mia glanced up and watched the one-sided dog-fight as another burning plane fell from the sky. She hoped Wicked Tina was right about the armed forces sorting it all out, but if that was the best they could offer they would be in for a long wait. The RAF planes were vastly outnumbered now, and as far as she could tell none of the flying saucers had even been harmed. Of the army there was no sign, but even if they did arrive soon Mia didn't think there would be much they could do to help.

She let out the clutch and followed Wicked Tina, keeping an eye on the Angels overhead. Only three planes still remained to put up a token resistance; the others lay in smoking rubble dotted around the landscape. She knew it wouldn't be long before the Angels turned their attention back to the fleeing motorcycles. She just hoped they would be far enough away by then, and out of sight from above, otherwise they wouldn't make it another mile, never mind thirty.

16

Footsteps clumped toward the staff room door. Mia stood up and joined the other women as they prepared to attack. A key rattled in the lock. The door handle depressed. The door opened slowly with a faint creak.

Mia grabbed the handle and yanked the door open fully. At the same time, Fat Brenda sprang forward to grab the soldier and drag him inside so he could be dealt with.

A metal tray containing cups and bowls fell clattering, spilling steaming hot food and drink everywhere. A female voice squealed in surprise. Mia closed the door and leaned against it to stop anyone else getting inside. Fat Brenda slammed the woman against the wall and held her in place with one meaty arm around her neck while she drew back a fist with the other.

"Don't hurt me," the woman cried, her voice squeaky with fear.

Except it wasn't a woman, Mia could see that now. She was just a girl, no more than thirteen or fourteen, and she was heavily pregnant. The huge distended stomach on such a tiny frame made her look like she had swallowed a football, while the short brown hair and NHS spectacles hanging from a chain around her neck made her look like an apprentice librarian.

"Who the hell are you?" Wicked Tina asked.

The girl trembled, her eyes darting around the room as she looked at each of the women in turn. "Di— Diana," she said. "I brung you something to eat." She looked down at the broken crockery and spillages. "But I dropped it. I'm really sorry, if you let me go I can fetch you some more?"

Fat Brenda lowered her fist and glared into the girl's face. "Who are those men who brought us here, and what do they want with us?"

"Why, they— they're soldiers, of course. They've saved you."

"Saved us for what?"

The girl's forehead furrowed. She blinked rapidly and rubbed her nose with one finger. "How do you mean?"

"I mean what do they want with us?"

"They want to save you. That's what they do. They're soldiers. They save people."

Fat Brenda raised her fist once more and drew it back. "Now look, you either give me some proper answers or I ram this down your throat. Your choice, bitch."

Diana burst into tears and her head dropped down.

"Let me have a go," Mia said.

Fat Brenda sighed and released her grip. "Be my guest."

Diana slumped to her knees and sobbed into her hands. Mia crouched before her and lifted her chin so she could make eye contact.

"Diana," she said softly, "do you see the cuts and bruises we have? Those soldiers did that to us, and—"

"No!" Diana shook her head. "They wouldn't do that. They're soldiers. They save people."

"They did. They hurt us. They also threatened to kill us if we didn't go with them. And then they locked us in this room. All we want to know is why we are here."

"To keep you safe, of course."

"Safe from who?"

"From the Angels." She bit her lip. "They went bad, started killing people. The soldiers saved us, then they chased them all away."

Mia nodded. "Okay, that was good of them. So how many of you are there? Not counting the soldiers, I mean."

"Well there's me, Maisy, Annabelle, Trisha, Sue and Dixie, we're all Badgers together. Then Kate and Jenny, they were already here when we came. So that's eight of us in total."

"What do you mean, you're all badgers?"

"That's what we call our Six. I'm the Sixer on account of being the oldest, Maisy is the Seconder. We were camping in the woods with Brown Owl when the Angels went bad. We had a pow-wow, but couldn't decide what to do so Brown Owl took over. She taught us what was safe to eat, and how to hide from the Angels so they couldn't get us."

Mia frowned. None of what the girl said made any sense. She looked at the others, who had crowded round to listen, to see if they had any ideas.

"They're Brownies," Suzy said. Everyone turned to gape at her. She shrugged. "What? My parents forced me into it when I was little, I had no bloody choice did I?"

Mia smiled and shook her head. She just couldn't imagine someone like Suzy ever being a Brownie. She turned back to Diana. "So this brown owl you were in the woods with, I'm guessing that would be your leader? Where is she now?"

Tears welled up in the girl's eyes again. "Brown Owl got sick a few days after we came here with the soldiers. Sergeant Harper kept her away from us so we wouldn't get sick too, but ... well, there's no hospitals any more you see, and she ... well, she's in heaven now."

"I'm sorry to hear that, Diana. The other girls, are they all the same age as you?"

"Kate and Jenny are a bit older I think, but not as old as you. We don't see them much though, they have their babies to look after." She rubbed her stomach affectionately and smiled. "I'll be joining them soon, though. You know, in the nursery?"

"Who's the father, honey?" Wicked Tina asked.

The girl looked at her and smiled. "Sergeant Harper. He's their leader, so I was really lucky he chose me."

"Bloody pervert," Suzy said. "He needs bloody castrating and shit if you ask me."

Mia shushed her and turned her attention back to the girl. "Listen, Diana, we want to leave here, can you help us?"

"No, you can't do that," Diana said quickly. "Sergeant Harper says it's all of our duty to repopulate the country. You've got to stay and help too, do your part. They won't like it if you say no. Dixie said no, and then they hit her, and made her do it anyway."

"Listen to me, Diana, we've got a much more important job to do." She pointed at Fat Brenda. "You see that big scary one there? She's our Brown Owl, and she's leading us on a mission to kill the Angels."

Fat Brenda stifled a smirk, but didn't contradict Mia. She turned away from the girl so she wouldn't see her crack into a wide grin.

Mia continued. "So it's your duty as fellow Brownies to help us get away from here so we can continue with our mission."

"Are you really Brownies?" Diana asked.

Suzy held up three fingers, her little finger tucked under her thumb. "I promise that I will do my best, be true to myself, and develop my beliefs ..."

"... to serve the Queen and my community, help other people, and keep the Brownie law," Diana continued, echoing Suzy's hand gesture. She looked at Mia expectantly. Mia arranged her fingers into the required position and held them up. The girl nodded. "Okay, so what do you need me to do?"

"How many soldiers are there?" Mia asked.

"Twelve, including Sergeant Harper," Diana said without a pause.

"And where are they now?"

"They're in the dining hut, it's supper time. We always have supper together every night. Even Kate and Jenny and their babies."

"Do they know you're here?"

"No, I sneaked out to bring you some food. They were going to let you go hungry, but that's not right is it? Everyone has to eat, don't they?"

Mia smiled. "Yes, they do. Thank you for that, Diana. Sorry we made you drop it."

"That's okay, I can easy get you some more. It's rabbit stew today, and there's plenty."

"We're not hungry right now, but thanks anyway. Listen, do you know where the soldiers keep their guns?"

"They have them all the time, in case the Angels come back."

"Do they have any spares?"

The girl nodded. "Yes, but we're not allowed to go near them, it's too dangerous."

"Can you show us where they are? We'll be really careful."

Diana frowned, then nodded. "I suppose."

"Good girl." Mia turned to Fat Brenda. "Brown Owl, what are your orders?"

Fat Brenda shrugged. "Let's go and have a look."

Wicked Tina opened the staff room door a small crack and peered out into the gift shop before opening it fully and stepping through.

Diana led them out of the gift shop and across the car park to the wooden huts. The sound of laughter came from one of the larger buildings, which Mia assumed must be the dining hut. They crept by it, ducking down as they passed the windows, and headed on to a smaller hut with what sounded like the steady thrum of an idling motorcycle engine coming from behind it. As they passed, Mia saw it was a petrol-powered electricity generator. Yellow in colour, with thick cables trailing from it into each of the wooden buildings.

A little further on they came to a large, windowless storage shed. An iron hasp with a large brass padlock held the door secure.

"They keep the spare guns in there," Diana said, pointing. She looked around nervously. "I'll have to get back now, otherwise they might miss me."

"Thank you, Diana," Mia said. "Don't tell anyone about this, will you? It's a Brownie secret."

"I won't."

After she had gone, Wicked Tina took out her dagger and hacked at the wood surrounding the hasp. She used the palm of her hand to hammer the blade in, then prised off small splinters to dig beneath it. Meanwhile, Margot and Suzy walked around the shed looking for another way inside.

Mia turned to Fat Brenda. "We should do something to help those kids before we go."

"Why?"

"Are you kidding? Those soldiers are raping them."

Fat Brenda shrugged. "Yeah well, maybe they are, maybe they aren't. Either way, it's none of our business. And that Diana, she seemed happy enough about it. Anyway, I was shagging around at her age, and I bet you were, too."

"Not with blokes nearly three times my age, I wasn't."

"Yeah well, it's not like there's anything we can do about it anyway, is there?"

"We could get them somewhere safe, somewhere those men couldn't get at them."

"And how long do you think they would last if we did that? At least here they get fed and kept alive. Out there on their own they wouldn't last more than a week."

Mia knew Fat Brenda was right, but she didn't like it one bit. She fought down the urge to slap the woman for her uncaring attitude and turned back to watch Wicked Tina's progress with the door. Margot and Suzy finished their circuit of the shed and reported there were no other ways inside, but Wicked

Tina had already chiselled a big enough gap under the hasp to loop her leather belt around it. Margot helped her tug on it, and the hasp creaked and groaned, then sprang free. Wicked Tina slung her belt over one shoulder and pulled the door open.

Inside were boxes of ammunition piled up high against the back wall, with rifles and submachine guns propped up against them. Hanging from rusty nails by their trigger guards were dozens of pistols and handguns. In one corner stood what looked like either a rocket-launcher or a bazooka, and in another several boxes of grenades.

Wicked Tina whistled. "Holy shit."

Margot smiled and rubbed her hands together as she walked into the shed. She picked up one of the rifles and sighted along it, then tossed it out to Suzy. Suzy caught it in one hand and passed it to Mia, then entered the shed and picked up one of the submachine guns.

"Now this is more like it," she said with a grin.

"Get the rest of them," Fat Brenda said. "And find out what type of bullets they take and get as many of those as you can carry. Get some of the little guns too." She followed Suzy, Wicked Tina and Margot into the shed, plucked one of the pistols from the wall, and stuffed it into her leather jacket pocket with the handle poking out.

Mia looked down at the rifle in her hands. It had what looked like an extra handle in front of the trigger guard, and when she yanked it off she found it was filled with large brass bullets. She snapped it back into place and inspected the rest of the gun. It had a short wooden stock, and a sight at the end of its black metal barrel. She lifted the rifle to her shoulder and squinted down the sight.

The door to the dining hut opened and a man in army fatigues staggered out. Mia watched, covering him with the rifle, as he leaned against the side of the hut with one hand and fumbled with the flies of his combat trousers. He sighed loudly while he urinated, waving his penis around to draw steaming circles on the hut's wooden wall. He turned toward Mia as he shook himself dry, then stared at her, bleary-eyed, for several seconds as if he were trying to figure out whether she was really there or not.

"Oi!" he shouted eventually, stuffing his penis away quickly.

Then he reached into his combat jacket with one hand.

Mia aimed at his chest and pulled the trigger. Nothing happened. The trigger was stuck in place and wouldn't move.

"What the hell?" she said, looking down at the rifle.

The man pulled out a pistol and waved it in Mia's general direction. He fired, but his aim was way off and the bullet thudded harmlessly into the storage shed wall several feet away from her. The man swore and covered one eye with a hand. He aimed again, and this time the gun pointed directly at Mia. She spun around, ready to dive through the storage shed door.

And came face to face with the barrel of another rifle.

"Move!" Wicked Tina yelled.

Mia ducked down. Wicked Tina fired, the sudden loud blast of the rifle leaving Mia's ears ringing.

A large hole punched through the man's stomach and blood spattered against the wall. His mouth gaped open. He dropped to his knees, still clutching the pistol, staring at Wicked Tina through wide, terrified eyes. Wicked Tina fired again and took off the top of his head, sending him sprawling onto his back.

"You've got your safety catch on, honey," Wicked Tina said, pointing at the side of her rifle above the trigger guard. "There's a little lever here you need to slide back."

Mia looked at her own rifle and found the lever. She twisted it with her thumb and nodded her thanks.

More men streamed out of the dining hut in a lurching manner, brandishing rifles and handguns. Mia and Wicked Tina both fired at the doorway at the same time. One man shrieked and crumpled to the ground when his kneecap exploded. The others scattered, leaving him behind. Some darted back inside, while others ran into the woodland, firing from the hip as they went. Bullets splintered into the shed's walls and kicked up dirt at Mia's feet. From inside the dining hut she could hear girls screaming in terror, men shouting at them to be quiet.

Margot, Fat Brenda and Suzy burst out of the storage shed with submachine guns. They fired into the woods, spraying bullets blindly in a wide arc, their arms vibrating from the guns' recoil. A man screamed. Another shouted an order to take cover. A bearded face appeared briefly at the dining hut door, low down near the ground. A hand reached out to the man with the shattered kneecap. Mia fired at the face and it disappeared back inside. She aimed at the screeching man on the ground and shot him between the legs. His screams reached a new crescendo as he writhed in agony, blood pooling around him.

Then a volley of shots came from the trees and pinged into the dirt all around her.

"Behind the shed, quick," Fat Brenda ordered.

Margot and Fat Brenda sprayed more bullets into the trees where the shots had come from while Mia, Suzy and Wicked Tina darted behind the shed. Margot and Fat Brenda backed up to join them, still firing as they went. Another man cried out in pain, but the returning barrage of fire continued. The women flattened themselves against the rear wall of the shed while bullets pinged into the ground either side of it.

"Shit," Margot said. "We can't stay here for long, sooner or later they'll hit one of those grenades and we'll all be blown to hell."

"Yeah well, we can't exactly go out there either, can we?" Fat Brenda said. "Besides, if all their extra guns and spare ammo are in that shed I can't see them wanting to blow it all up."

The firing stopped, as if the men had suddenly realised the same thing. Fat Brenda peered around the corner of the shed, then ducked back when another shot splintered wood inches from her head.

"Give me a bunk-up," Suzy said.

Fat Brenda looked at her. "You what?"

"We need to see what they're up to. If I get on the roof I might be able to see where they are."

"That's a hell of a risk," Mia said. "They'll see you straight away."

"Maybe not, if I stay flat."

Fat Brenda nodded. "Do it. But if they see you, get back down here straight away."

Wicked Tina clasped her hands before her and Suzy stepped onto them and hauled herself up. She tossed her submachine gun onto the shed's roof and reached up to curl her fingers over the edge. Mia grabbed her flailing boot and helped Wicked Tina push her higher. Suzy managed to get her elbows onto the roof and squirmed her way up, her feet kicking. As soon as she was up on the roof, her gun rattled out dozens of rapid-fire shots.

"Two of the bastards were trying to sneak up on us from the bloody dining hut," she said. "Anyone know how many are left in there now?"

Mia tried to think how many she had seen run back into the hut, but it had all happened too fast to take any notice of small details like that.

"Never mind," Suzy said, "I can see one at the window now. He's holding one of the girls in front of him."

"Kill the bastard," Fat Brenda said.

"No," Mia said quickly, "you might hit the girl."

Suzy's gun fired in a two-second burst.

"No!" Mia shouted. She punched the wall of the shed and swore.

"Got another one," Suzy said calmly. "Girl seems okay, just a bit hysterical." Then: "Shit! There's three more of them coming from the woods!"

A new sustained hail of bullets thudded into the storage shed. Suzy scrambled across its roof and jumped down next to Wicked Tina. Fat Brenda screamed a war cry and stepped away from the shed wall, firing her submachine gun in a continuous burst. She arced it across the clearing, aiming for the trees, giving Margot enough covering fire to take out one of the three men running straight at them. He jiggled and danced like an epileptic marionette as Margot's spray of bullets almost cut him in half at the chest, then fell back in a bloody mess. Mia took out one of the others with a shot to the neck that sent arterial blood spraying. The man fell to his knees screaming, and clutched his neck with both hands in a futile attempt to stop the life-force pumping from it.

Margot aimed for the remaining man and fired. He ducked and rolled just in time, bullets whizzing over his head. He continued rolling over and over, like a kid rolling down a hill, toward the dining hut. Margot fired again, but he was already out of her line of sight. More shots from the trees around the clearing stopped her from pursuing him.

A single shot rang out from behind and something warm and wet splattered onto the back of Mia's neck. She clasped her neck instinctively and spun around just in time to see Suzy collapse forwards, the top of her head missing. Brains and splinters of shattered skull slopped onto the ground by Mia's feet.

"Suzy!" Mia shouted, and dropped to her knees by the corpse of her friend.

She startled when Wicked Tina placed a hand on her shoulder. She looked up, tears rolling down her face.

Wicked Tina raised her rifle and ducked down behind Mia, firing off two shots into the nearby woodland.

"There's someone behind us!" she shouted.

Fat Brenda kept up her volley of shots at the front of the shed, while Margot ran to the rear. She glanced down at Suzy's body, swore, then peered down her submachine gun into the trees.

"Where is he?" she asked, waving the gun from side to side.

Wicked Tina pointed. "I saw one duck behind that tree, I reckon he's still there."

"Any others?"

"Don't know, I just saw one. The bastard killed Suzy."

Margot nodded grimly. "Yeah, I know. And we'll get him for that, don't you worry. Go and see if you can draw him out, I'll cover you from here."

"No," Mia said, picking up Suzy's fallen submachine gun. "I'll do this. Tina, you make sure nobody comes out of that dining hut."

Wicked Tina nodded, then walked around the back of the storage shed and covered the dining hut with her rifle. Mia set off toward the trees while Margot sprayed bullets into the trunk of the one Wicked Tina had indicated the man stood behind. Mia ducked low as she hobbled from tree to tree, circling around the woodland to take the man by surprise while Margot kept him pinned down. She dropped to her hands and knees, ignoring the pain the impact against her injury caused, and crawled through bushes, out the other side, and sprinted to another tree. She took a quick glance around it, then ducked back when she saw him. It was Anderson, holding a sniper rifle by his side. He faced the tree, standing straight, using the tree's massive trunk to shield him from Margot's sporadic fire. Mia limped toward him, fresh blood from her grazed knees dribbling down her legs, the submachine gun trained on the sniper's back the whole time.

"Hey Anderson!" she shouted when she was six feet away.

Anderson startled and spun toward her, raising his rifle.

Mia pulled the trigger and held it in place. The gun juddered in her hands as dozens of rapid-fire bullets tore into Anderson's stomach. His body jerked with involuntary muscle spasms, the air filled with the sound of his screams. Mia released the trigger and watched him fall to his knees, blood pouring from a huge gaping hole in his stomach. He clutched it with one hand while he tried to raise the rifle in the other.

Mia aimed at the hand holding the rifle and fired a short burst. Arterial blood spurted as the hand disintegrated into a mass of ruined flesh and sinew. The rifle dropped. Anderson glared at her defiantly, his teeth clenched in pain.

"That's for Suzy," Mia said, limping toward him. She kicked him in the face and sent him sprawling onto his back. "And this," she said, stepping over him, "is for what you've been doing to those little girls." She pointed the gun down at Anderson's face and pulled the trigger.

Back at the huts, a male voice shouted something, but Mia couldn't make out the words over the ringing in her ears and the sound of sporadic gunfire coming from that direction. She wiped blood and bits of Anderson's flesh from her motorcycle boots on a tuft of grass and picked up the fallen sniper rifle. She raised it and looked through the telescopic sight to see what was going on.

Sergeant Harper stood by the side of the dining hut, one arm around Diana's neck, a pistol pointed at her head. He crouched behind her, using her as a human shield. Two more men with rifles flanked him. Mia made her way closer, darting from tree to tree, the sniper rifle held in one hand, the submachine gun in the other.

"You think we care what you do to her?" Fat Brenda shouted.

"Oh, I think you do," Harper said. "Besides, you have my word that I will let you walk out of here with your lives if you give yourselves up."

Fat Brenda snorted. "Yeah, like that's going to happen."

"Look, we've both suffered casualties here. So we can either carry on killing each other, or we can end this now. It's your choice."

Mia crept closer and took up a position behind a tree not far from where Harper stood. She propped the submachine gun up against the tree trunk and squinted through the rifle's sight. Harper's grinning face filled the viewfinder. She lined up the crosshairs on his forehead. It would be so easy to just blow him away. With a gun like this it would be impossible to miss. She breathed in deep through her mouth, filling her lungs with oxygen. Her finger curled over the trigger. Then she hesitated. If her hand jerked with the shot and she missed by just a few inches she might kill Diana. Could she take that risk? And what if the viewfinder wasn't even accurate? There was no real way of knowing without firing a test shot, and that would betray her position in the woods.

Margot and Fat Brenda stepped out from either side of the storage shed, their submachine guns pointing down. The two men with rifles turned to aim at them.

"Wise choice," Harper said, smiling. "But where's the others?"

"They're all dead, you bastard," Fat Brenda said in a monotone.

Mia's stomach flipped. She spun the sniper rifle's sight to the storage shed in search of Wicked Tina, but there was no sign of her. She choked back a sob. Those bastards in the woods must have shot her, too. She trained the sniper rifle back on Harper. He would pay for that, just as soon as she could get a clear shot at him without putting the girl in danger.

"Ah, that's unfortunate," Harper said. "But like I say, we've both suffered casualties here. Now throw your weapons away and get down on your knees."

Margot and Fat Brenda looked at each other. Fat Brenda nodded. They both dived for the ground simultaneously, firing their submachine guns at the two men either side of Harper. Both men fell under a hail of bullets, their rifles clattering away from them.

Then Wicked Tina stepped out from behind the storage shed and sauntered toward Harper, her rifle trained on him.

"I really wish you hadn't done that," Harper said, his pistol still held against the side of Diana's head. He grinned and pulled the trigger. Diana's eyes bulged a split second before her head exploded outwards. Harper dropped her limp body and spun to point his pistol at Wicked Tina.

"No!" Mia screamed. She ran forward, the pain in her knees forgotten.

Wicked Tina shot first, closely followed by Margot and Fat Brenda. Harper jerked as bullets tore through him and sprayed the wall of the dining hut with splatters of blood. Fat Brenda continued firing long after there was any point to it, pumping round after round into his quivering body until it was reduced to a bloody mess.

Mia fell to a sprawl beside Diana's corpse and sobbed as she stared at it. If only she'd been brave enough to take that shot she could have saved the girl's life. Her unborn baby too.

"I'm so sorry," she spluttered. "This is all my fault."

Diana's stomach seemed to twitch beneath her bloodstained dress. Mia stared, unable to believe her own eyes. It just wasn't possible. She had already decided it was just a trick of the mind when there was another faint flutter of movement. Mia ripped Diana's dress open and placed a hand over her distended stomach. It moved again, like something brushing against the underside of the girl's skin.

"Quick, Tina, give me your dagger," she shouted, taking off her leather jacket.

Wicked Tina looked at her sharply. "You what?"

"Your dagger, quick. The baby's still alive in there. We need to get it out before it dies."

"Are you kidding, honey? Do you even know how to do that?"

"No, but I have to try. I'm not going to let another baby die, not if I can help it."

Wicked Tina took the dagger from her boot and handed it to Mia. "What do you mean, *another* baby?"

"Nothing, forget it. I'll tell you later."

Mia gripped the dagger with one hand and felt along Diana's stomach with the other, trying to pinpoint where the baby was so she wouldn't slice into it. She positioned the tip of the serrated blade just below the girl's chest and punctured the skin, then drew the blade slowly down her stomach until she got close to where she judged the baby's head to be. She stopped, withdrew the dagger, then returned to the start of the incision to cut deeper. Blood pooled around the jagged gash as she cut through fatty tissue and muscle. She put down the dagger and pushed her fingers into the wound, prised the flesh apart with a ripping sound, and reached inside for the baby. She cupped her hand over the baby's head, up to her elbow in gore, and told Wicked Tina to continue cutting.

Wicked Tina swore as she picked up the blood-stained dagger. Under Mia's direction she sliced across Diana's chest, carving the dead girl open like a Sunday joint. Mia felt the blade nick her arm as she cut deeper, and told her to stop. Wicked Tina leaned back and watched while Mia tore the flesh open with her hands. She could see the baby's face, encased in some kind of membrane filled with fluid. She reached in further and gripped the baby by its chest, then tugged. Warm fluid spurted up into her face as the membrane ruptured, the rest pouring out of the girl's ruined body and splashing over Mia's knees. She pulled harder as the warm fluid dripped from her chin, and felt something give way just before the baby came free with a wet slurping sound.

It was still and lifeless, its skin an unnatural blue in tone, slick with amniotic fluid and specks of blood. Remnants of membrane clung to its face and upper chest. The umbilical cord trailed back into Diana's butchered remains, a mottled grey in colour.

Mia put the baby down on the soft lining of her leather jacket and peeled the membrane from its face. She prised its mouth open and inserted her finger, used it to scoop out the remaining membrane and amniotic fluid. The baby felt deathly cold to the touch. She picked it up and cradled it in one arm, then lifted her T-shirt and placed it against her warm, bare skin and gently rubbed its back with the palm of her hand.

"Come on, come on," she said. "Breathe, you bastard."

"You need to hold it upside down and slap its arse," Wicked Tina said. "I saw them do it on a telly show once."

"Are you sure?" Mia looked up and saw a group of seven young girls staring down at her, open-mouthed in horror. Two of them were heavily pregnant, others only just starting to show.

Wicked Tina shrugged. "That's what I saw them do, and it seemed to work then."

Mia nodded. It was worth a try, and she didn't have any alternative ideas of her own. She took hold of the baby's ankles, ready to pull it out and swing it upside down so she could slap it. The baby seemed to convulse, then fluid shot from its mouth and dribbled down Mia's arm. Then it let out a screeching wail and flailed its arms, its tiny fists clenched. Mia smiled down at it through the neck of her T-shirt and tickled its chin with her finger. She thought about her baby sister, how she had died because of her, and vowed nothing like that would ever happen again. This time she would protect the baby, save it from harm. Defend it with her life if she had to.

"You'll need to tie the cord off before you cut it," Wicked Tina said. "I'll go and see if I can find some string or something."

Mia nodded.

"Is that how all babies come out?" one of the heavily pregnant young girls asked. Her bottom lip trembled as she gaped at Diana's ruined body.

Mia shook her head. "No. No, of course not. Don't worry, I'll look after you when the time comes."

"Will it hurt?"

Mia didn't know what to say. The girl was already terrified, and she didn't want to upset her any further by telling her the truth. She smiled. "You'll be fine, I promise."

PART 4

THE FINAL SHOWDOWN

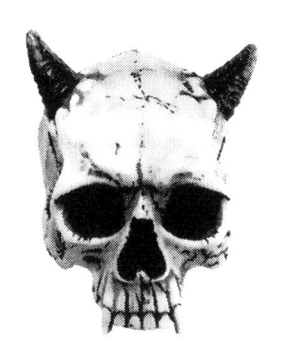

17

Mia couldn't help smiling while she watched the baby in her arms suckling on a bottle of ready-made milk formula. The soldiers had stockpiled thousands of such bottles in one of the huts, along with dozens and dozens of terry cloth nappies and sets of baby clothes, and for that she was eternally grateful because she wouldn't know where to start looking for such things herself.

Mia had moved into the hut the girls shared together, taking up Diana's vacant bed, on the night the baby was born. In the three days since, she had seen very little of Margot and Fat Brenda, and only sporadic visits from Wicked Tina, with most of her time taken up with looking after the baby and trying to reassure the other girls they had nothing to worry about now the soldiers had all gone. So it was a surprise when she looked up from the baby and saw Fat Brenda standing in the hut's doorway, watching her intently.

"Don't get too attached to it," Fat Brenda said. "I'm here to tell you we're leaving in the morning."

"He's a *he*, not an *it*," Mia said, looking back down at the baby. "Aren't you, Little Bonehead?"

Fat Brenda snorted. "Little Bonehead? You're kidding, right?"

Mia pulled the bottle from the baby's mouth and propped him upright, then patted his back gently. He spat a mouthful of milk and belched.

"Don't you think he looks just like him? Without the beard, I mean."

Fat Brenda walked up to the baby and peered down at him. She shrugged. "Well it's bald and ugly, if that's what you mean. But all babies look like that."

Mia gasped in mock horror. "That's not right, is it, Little Bonehead?" she said to the baby, shaking her head and smiling. "Aunty Brenda's being a silly old cow, isn't she? You're a handsome little chap, and don't let anyone tell you otherwise."

"Christ," Fat Brenda said, "what the hell's wrong with you, Mia? You're talking like some sort of retard. It's not as if it can understand anything you say."

"You don't know that." Mia lay the baby back down on her arm and resumed feeding him.

"Yeah well, whatever. The truck's all loaded up, and first thing in the morning we're out of here. And we're not taking that thing with us, so you'll have to leave it here."

"And what if I say I don't want to go?"

"What? Of course you're going. You can't let us down now, not when we're this close."

"They're all dead, FB, and they're not coming back no matter what we do. Same goes for Suzy. Things have changed, now. There's people here who need us, we can't just go off and leave them to fend for themselves. Annabelle and Dixie will be having their babies soon, that's more important than some half-arsed scheme to kill a few Angels. Besides, we could make a proper life here. It's miles away from the nearest Angel patrol, so if we're careful they'd never even know we existed."

"What, so you'd rather stay here and settle down, play at being a good little citizen? What do you think Bonehead would have to say about that?"

"That's not fair."

Fat Brenda folded her arms. "Yeah well, it wasn't fair we had to bury Suzy without you because you didn't want that thing to catch a cold out in the open."

"Suzy would have understood."

"You know what, Mia?" Fat Brenda said, turning away. "You can do what the hell you like." She stormed out of the hut and slammed the door behind her.

"She's wrong, you know," Mia said to the baby. "Bonehead would have seen the sense in staying here; he was the one who convinced everyone we'd be safer staying put in the nature reserve instead of living on the road like we used to before. I wish you could have met him, Little Bonehead. He was kind and gentle, the most caring man I ever knew." Thoughts of Bonehead brought a lump to Mia's throat. She sighed and shook her head. "Anyway, let's get that nappy changed, shall we?"

Ten minutes later, after she successfully managed to fasten a terry cloth nappy onto the wriggling baby and re-dress him in his bright yellow dungarees, Mia heard a cry of alarm outside. She picked up the baby and hurried to the door, then swung it open and looked out. Jenny, one of the older girls, was in tears, being consoled by Annabelle and Maisy. Trisha, Sue, Kate and Dixie rushed out of the dining hut to join them.

"What's happened?" Kate asked.

"She saw someone in the woods," Maisy said.

Trisha and Sue both gasped. Mia looked beyond the huddle of girls and peered into the trees, looking for any sign of movement. Wicked Tina, lounging on the bonnet of the armoured jeep and sipping from a bottle of vodka, jumped off and reached through the passenger side window for one of the rifles propped up on the seat. She turned and aimed into the woods, scanning the thick line of trees. The baby, sensing a sudden change in mood, began to cry. Mia shushed him as she walked up to the girls.

"Who did you see?" she asked Kate, a sense of urgency in her voice.

Fat Brenda and Margot joined Wicked Tina by the side of the jeep and armed themselves with rifles.

Kate sniffled and wiped her nose with the back of her hand, smearing snot across her cheek. "I didn't say I *saw* someone, I said I *heard* someone. I didn't wait long enough to find out who it was."

"What did you hear?" Mia asked.

"I was picking mushrooms, and there was all these twigs snapping behind me. I thought it might be an Angel coming to get me, so I ran."

"There's no Angels here," Mia said, shaking her head. "It must have been an animal or something."

"Unless we missed one of those army bastards," Fat Brenda said. "We'd best go and have a look, just in case."

Mia tried to think if all the soldiers had been accounted for. There were twelve in total, Diana had said, and she ticked off the ones she knew for sure had been killed. That left one she couldn't be sure about. She remembered hearing his scream, but didn't know if anyone had bothered to look for his body after it was all over. Was it really possible one might be still alive out there, injured and looking for revenge? If there was, they were all in danger.

"Inside, quick!" she shouted, and herded the girls into the dining hut.

Margot, Fat Brenda and Wicked Tina spread out and walked into the woods, their guns pointing the way. Mia thought about going with them, but decided not to. If there really was a soldier out there in the woods, someone would need to stay behind and protect the girls from him. So she armed herself with a submachine gun from the back of the truck before joining the girls in the dining hut. She gave the baby to Maisy, barricaded the door with tables and chairs, and stared through one of the windows with the submachine gun ready in case the soldier made a dash for them.

After an anxious half hour wait, Fat Brenda, Margot and Wicked Tina returned from the woods.

"Can't find anyone," Fat Brenda said when Mia shot her a quizzical glance through the window. "Saw a deer though, so maybe that was what she heard."

"Did you see any bodies?" Mia asked.

"Only the ones we dragged into the woods." She smiled. "Looks like something's been chewing on them."

"You think there might still be another one out there?"

"I doubt it, he'd have shown himself by now if there was. A trained soldier wouldn't be stamping about like that anyway, he'd look where he was walking. And he'd be more likely to shoot from a distance than try sneak up on someone."

Mia nodded. "Yeah. Yeah, you're right."

But a tiny niggle of doubt remained in Mia's mind, so when she retired for the evening she took the submachine gun with her and propped it up against the Moses basket by the side of her bed. Little Bonehead, wide awake, gurgled up at her as she drifted off to sleep.

She dreamed of riding pillion on Bonehead's motorcycle, her arms clutched around his chest, her cheek resting against the back of his sleeveless denim jacket. Little Bonehead, dressed in a tiny leather jacket with Satan's Bastards insignia painted on the back, sat in a sidecar to her right. It was his first ride, and Mia could tell he loved every second of it from the wide grin on his face.

They were on their way to a music festival, and she couldn't wait to get there. Couldn't wait to show Little Bonehead off to the rest of Satan's Bastards when they met up at Stonehenge, and introduce him to the joys of Hawkwind and Pink Floyd.

Bonehead twisted the throttle and accelerated hard. Little

Bonehead squealed in delight and flapped his arms as if he were flying. Mia stretched out her arms like the wings of an aeroplane and laughed along with him.

Then Bonehead twisted himself around in the saddle, grabbed her feet, and yanked her into a prone position before climbing on top of her.

"Stupid bitch!" he said. "You think you're better than me?"

Mia startled awake in pitch darkness. She tried to sit up, but someone was straddled over her, pinning her down just like Bonehead had been doing in her dream.

The soldier! He must have sneaked in during the night.

Mia gasped in air, an involuntary cry of alarm on her lips. A rough hand forced a wet cloth over her nose and mouth. She could taste chloroform, and felt its vapours sting her eyes. She held her breath and tried to prise the hand away from her mouth, digging her fingernails into her attacker's wrist as she tugged against it, but it wouldn't budge. She thrashed on the bed, kicking out wildly to free herself. Two hands clamped over her nose and mouth and forced her head deeper into the pillow. Her mind screamed for oxygen. Stars popped before her eyes. She swung a fist and felt it connect with something soft, but there was little power behind it.

Her lungs were on fire. She couldn't hold out any longer. Just one tiny breath, then she'd be able to fight back. Free herself, then grab the gun beside the bed and blow him away. She sucked in a gasp of air through the chloroform-soaked cloth. Her head swam. She could feel herself spinning slowly, could hear a faint buzzing sound in her ears, the rasping breath of her assailant beginning to echo as all her muscles relaxed as one. Her body took over, instinct forcing more chloroform into her lungs. Deep, slow breaths.

Then she was gone, her mind and body spinning out of control. Back into her dreams. Into the arms of Bonehead, so soft and reassuring. She wished she could stay there forever.

18

So far, each time Mia had stirred a fresh dose of chloroform had sent her spinning back to unconsciousness. This time she was determined to lie still, keep her breathing deep and regular until she had all her wits about her and could figure out what to do. Her mouth felt dry and furry, like the morning after a heavy drinking session. The cold metal floor rattled beneath her, like someone kept hitting it from below with a hammer in rhythm with the pounding in her head. She lay on her side, one knee bent to stop her rolling onto her stomach, her head resting on one arm while her other arm splayed out before her. The roar of an engine filled her ears. She lay in a moving vehicle, that much was obvious. But going where? And who had taken her? The soldier?

Mia risked a quick glance and opened one eye. It looked like the army truck Anderson and the others had bundled them into when they were taken to the visitor centre. But if it was the same truck, who was driving? One soldier couldn't drive and administer chloroform at the same time, so there would need to be at least two of them. Had reinforcements arrived from somewhere? Another patrol out looking for women? But that wouldn't explain why she was alone in the truck.

Boxes of ammunition and hand grenades lay beneath the bench at the side of the truck. They looked like the ones from the storage shed Margot and Wicked Tina had loaded into their own truck the previous day. So maybe there would be guns too? If she could reach one of them in time she might be able to take her captor by surprise, then that would just leave the driver to take care of. She cast her eyes as far down the length of the truck as she could without moving her head. Yes, there was guns. Lots of guns. But all of them too far away to reach in time.

She listened, trying to ignore the roar of the engine and the rattle of the truck as it drove over potholes in the road. She could hear someone breathing heavily behind her, the occasional shuffle of feet. He must be sitting on the bench on the opposite side. If Mia tried to reach one of the guns he'd be on her in an instant. Her best bet would be to get him to come closer, catch him off guard and overpower him.

Mia murmured and twitched her fingers, straightened her bent leg and let out a low moan as if she were only just coming round from the chloroform. The man behind her grunted in reply, then the truck rocked slightly as he stood up. Mia moaned again and rolled onto her back and opened her eyes a tiny crack. A silhouette crouched over her. Chloroform vapours filled her nostrils. A hand reached down. Mia swatted it away, then twisted her body and threw a punch at the man's torso. It sank in deep, and he let out a gasping oof as he doubled up in pain and staggered back. The bottle of chloroform fell and rolled across the floor of the truck, spilling its contents. Mia sprang up, ready to press home her advantage and pulverise the bastard.

Fat Brenda stood before her, palms held out in surrender, a pained expression on her face.

"What the hell?" Mia said. "*You* did this to me?" She clenched her fists and raised them, ready to do some serious damage to Fat Brenda's face if she didn't get a sensible answer from the woman.

"It's for your own good, Mia." Fat Brenda slumped down on the bench. She shrugged, palms still held up. "You can hit me again if it makes you feel any better, but if you miss out on this you'll regret it for the rest of your life, and you know it."

"Miss out on what?"

"Closure. Revenge. Killing Angels. Whatever you want to call it."

Mia shook her head. "Take me back, right now. I don't want any part in this, and you know that."

"It's too late for that, we're already nearly there."

"Bullshit. It'd take days to travel that far." Fat Brenda shrugged again. Mia felt her knees weaken, the effects of her adrenalin rush wearing off. She sat down on the bench opposite Fat Brenda and nodded slowly. "That's how long you've kept me out of it, isn't it?"

"I did it for you, can't you see that? Once it's all over, you'll thank me."

"The hell I will. So who else is in on this?"

"Me and Margot agreed it was the right thing to do. She's the one driving."

"And Tina?"

"She's following in the jeep. She doesn't know you're here yet, she thinks we left you behind."

Mia closed her eyes and held her head in her hands. Who the hell did Margot and Fat Brenda think they were, kidnapping her like this? Who was looking after Little Bonehead in her absence? And what if there really was another soldier out there in the woods? Those girls would have been left defenceless.

She had to get back there somehow, before anything bad happened to any of them. She couldn't handle another dead baby on her conscience, not after what happened to her sister. She sighed and looked up, meeting Fat Brenda's cold stare.

"Okay, here's what's going to happen. As soon as we stop I'm taking the jeep and going back to Northumberland. The rest of you can do whatever you want, but it's all over for me. And if anything's happened to Little Bonehead while I've been away I'm going to come back here and kill you. Very slowly. You got that, FB?"

Fat Brenda nodded, smiling. "Yeah, whatever. You'll feel differently once we get there, you'll see."

Mia sighed. "Is there anything to eat? I'm starving."

19

The truck lurched to a halt with a hiss of hydraulic brakes. Mia glared at Fat Brenda while they both waited for Margot to open the rear door and let them out. Fat Brenda jumped down first and took Margot to one side, then whispered something into her ear. Margot glanced at Mia and nodded, then disappeared from view. When Mia climbed out she saw her give the truck's keys to Fat Brenda. She must have warned her about Mia's plans to leave, and wanted to make sure she didn't take the truck with her. Well that was fine, it was the jeep she wanted anyway.

They were on a straight, narrow country road, green hills either side of them. The road stretched for miles in both directions with nothing else man-made in sight — not even any electricity pylons or telegraph poles, which Mia had always assumed would be everywhere. She wondered why anyone would bother laying a road through such a place. Why would anyone want to come here? As far as she could tell, the road only led to the base of a snow-topped mountain on the horizon, hardly much of a destination for tourists and sightseers.

Mia shivered in the cold wind and blew on her hands while she watched Wicked Tina approach from the distance. "What have you stopped here for?" she asked Margot.

"This is as close as we can get by road."

"As close to what?"

"Where the Angels go at night." Margot pointed left. "We reckon they're somewhere over that way. See that big rock on top of that hill? They disappeared behind that last night, so they can't be far away."

Mia cupped a hand over her eyes and looked, but there was nothing much to see. Just a big mound of overgrown grass with a huge boulder on top. How the boulder got up there, or why it was there, was anyone's guess.

Wicked Tina parked the jeep behind the truck and opened the door. "What are *you* doing here, honey?" she asked, staring at Mia.

"Ask them two."

Wicked Tina turned to Fat Brenda. "Well?"

Fat Brenda shrugged. "Mia's gone soft. She cares more about that stupid baby than she does about Satan's Bastards. We did what had to be done."

"They kidnapped me," Mia said. "Drugged me while I was asleep, then kept me prisoner in that truck."

Wicked Tina's eyes widened as they flicked back to Mia. "Seriously? Christ, I had no idea, honey." To Fat Brenda she said, "That's why you always insisted on getting the food from the truck yourself, isn't it? So I wouldn't find out. You knew I wouldn't have agreed to this."

Fat Brenda shrugged again. "Yeah well, she's here now, that's all that matters."

"Not for much longer I'm not," Mia said. "As soon as it gets dark I'm taking that jeep and pissing off back to Northumberland." To Wicked Tina she added, "You can come with me if you like. You'll only get yourself killed if you stay here."

"Nobody's going anywhere until this is finished with," Fat Brenda said, walking up to the jeep. She leaned inside and took the keys from the ignition, then pocketed them.

Mia took a step toward her, fists clenched. She needed those keys to get away. But before she could get any closer, Fat Brenda pulled a pistol out of her leather jacket and pointed it at her chest.

"What, you're going to shoot me now?" Mia shook her head. "That's the new Satan's Bastards way, is it? I'm sure Dirk would be very proud of you right now."

"Nobody's shooting anyone," Margot said. "Look, Mia, you can go tonight if that's really what you want. But until then you might as well stay with us. What's done is done, and there's no point sulking about it now."

"Fine," Mia said, still glaring at Fat Brenda. "So what have you got in mind?"

Fat Brenda put the pistol away. "We're going to walk up that hill and see what's on the other side of it. If that's where the Angels are we'll take it from there. If they're not, we'll wait until one flies over and see where it goes next."

"Why not just drive up there?" Wicked Tina asked. "It doesn't look too steep, and these things are designed for off-road, so they should be able to manage it easy enough."

"Try using your brain," Fat Brenda said. "If any Angels fly over they'd see us straight away. On foot we could hide in the grass."

Margot reached into the back of the truck and pulled out a sniper rifle and a submachine gun. She tossed the rifle to Wicked Tina, and surprised Mia by handing her the submachine gun before reaching back inside for two more. They each filled their pockets with spare ammunition, then Margot led the way down a short embankment into an overgrown field filled with thistles, dandelions and nettles. It was hard going, even harder when the ground began to slope up at the bottom of the hill and they had to lean forward to keep their balance. When they reached the boulder at the top they slumped against it and stared down at what lay on the other side of the hill.

The mangled remains of destroyed tanks, crashed planes, burnt-out personnel carriers, and other unidentifiable vehicles of war littered the ground for miles. Hundreds, possibly thousands of bodies lay between them, reduced to blackened bones and scraps of clothing. Mia shivered involuntarily at the sight. It reminded her of that night back at the nature reserve when they'd returned to find everyone dead, except this was a million times worse. All those lives wasted, and nobody to mourn for them. Not even anyone to give them a decent burial.

In the distance, inside a huge flat circular clearing, were what looked like blue metallic domes of a uniform size. Mia counted thirty-eight of them in total, arranged in a perfect circle, equidistant to each other.

"You see anything?" Fat Brenda asked.

Wicked Tina, looking through the scope of her sniper rifle, shook her head. "Not really, honey. Bunch of big round blue things, but no Angels anywhere."

"We should take a closer look," Margot said, and set off down the hill with Fat Brenda.

Mia glanced at Wicked Tina and frowned. "What do you think?"

Wicked Tina shrugged. "Might as well, now we're here."

Mia sighed. "Come on then. The sooner we get this done, the sooner I can get going back to Little Bonehead."

They zig-zagged their way down the hill to avoid the worst of the wreckage before them, and stepped gingerly over piles of human bones it wasn't possible to skirt around. Margot and Fat Brenda maintained their lead, and reached the flat ground first. They waited beside a burnt-out tank for Mia and Wicked Tina to catch up, then all four continued together.

While they were working their way around another tank, an Angel spaceship approached from the south. Mia heard it first, and pointed it out to the others. They watched it hover over the domes, then drop down between them. Seven minutes later if rose again and flew back south. The women continued closer to the domes once it was far enough away to notice them from the sky.

Four hundred yards from the closest of the domes they stopped and peered around the mangled remains of a fighter jet's fuselage jutting out of a small crater in the ground. The pilot's skeleton grinned out at them through the cockpit's shattered window. The wings were missing, as was the rear of the plane's body, just rusting, jagged metal to show they had ever existed.

Another Angel ship flew in from the south and hovered over the centre of the ring of domes. As it dropped down its distinctive hum cut away to silence. Seven Angels waddled toward it. Mia didn't see where they came from, but assumed they must have been inside the domes when it arrived. They faced the ship, their backs to Mia and the others.

The underside of the ship shimmered and something dropped from it. An Angel bent over it and scooped it up, then took it to one of the domes on the far side of the complex. An elongated oval section of the dome shimmered and the Angel and its burden disappeared inside. Seconds later the dome returned to its uniform metallic blue colour once more.

Something else dropped from the ship and an Angel picked it up and took it into the same dome. Then the saucer rose and the remaining Angels wandered away in separate directions. It was only when the ship reached a height of thirty feet that it began humming again, and Mia realised the whole scene up to that point had played out in absolute silence.

"What do you reckon that was about?" Wicked Tina asked, her voice barely a whisper as the flying saucer zipped away.

Fat Brenda shrugged. "Only one way to find out." She stepped out from behind the wrecked plane and walked closer to the domes, her submachine gun held by her side. "Wait here, I won't be long."

She got another hundred yards, then cried out and fell backwards, covering her nose with one hand. Blood poured between her fingers.

"What the hell?" Margot said, stepping forward.

Fat Brenda stood up and reached out tentatively before her. She seemed to hold the palm of her hand flat against the air, and when she lowered it a smear of blood floated before her. She drew back her submachine gun and jabbed it forward. Without any sound, it stopped dead in the same position as the floating blood smear, as if it had struck something solid.

"What is it?" Margot asked.

"Dunno." Fat Brenda stepped sideways, her hand held out before her, smearing more blood in the air. "It's warm, whatever it is."

Margot pressed her hand against the air, then formed a fist and thumped it three times. "Some sort of force-field, like the one around the ships? I guess that would explain why nobody got close enough to blow them up."

"Yeah well," Fat Brenda said, wiping blood from her nose. "There must be an opening somewhere, we just need to find it." She began walking, her arm stretched out by her side, her fingers trailing against ... nothing.

Mia and Wicked Tina walked over to the invisible barrier and felt it for themselves, then followed Fat Brenda and Margot. They walked in silence for half an hour, and still hadn't found a way inside when they reached the far side of the circle of domes.

"This is pointless," Mia said. "There's no way inside, so we might as well just go."

"Maybe it doesn't go very high up," Wicked Tina said. "I mean, they can fly in and out, right? And they've got them long legs of theirs, so they could just step over it? So I reckon maybe we could stand on something and climb over ourselves?"

Mia nodded, then picked up a small stone and threw it as

high as she could. It hit the barrier and bounced off before thudding to the ground.

"Or maybe not," Margot said.

"Yeah well," Fat Brenda said, raising her submachine gun, "let's see if it will stand up to this."

She fired a short burst point-blank at the force-field. Flattened bullets fell by her feet. Mia readied her own weapon, expecting to see hordes of Angels pouring out of the domes to investigate the sudden noise. But inside the barrier, nothing stirred.

Another flying saucer approached from the west at tremendous speed. The women darted behind a nearby tank as it flew closer, and watched it drop down between the domes. Mia crept to the edge of the tank and peered between two domes to get a better look as a group of Angels gathered around it.

A naked man fell from the underside of the ship and landed on his back. Mia thought he was dead at first, but then she saw him move. He raised his head and looked around in horror, then scrabbled backwards when an Angel lunged forward to grab him. His mouth opened in a silent scream, his eyes wide and staring. The Angel curled its long fingers over the man's head and lifted him from the ground. He swung in its grip, his legs kicking, his arms flailing as the Angel carried him out of view behind one of the domes. Another naked man fell, another Angel scooped him up and took him away. Then another. And another.

"Holy shit," Wicked Tina said. "They've got people in there."

Mia nodded, but she couldn't take her eyes off the flying saucer while another naked man fell from it. Her eyes widened as he sprang to his feet and ran.

"Go on, you can do it," she said, willing the man to get away.

Three Angels dropped down to all fours and gave chase. The man darted between domes, his arms pumping, running for his life. The Angels split up, flanking him like a pack of wild dogs chasing a rabbit. The man changed direction and hurtled closer to where Mia and Wicked Tina stood watching. He locked eyes with Mia and his mouth dropped open as he ran. The Angels closed in on him from three different directions.

"Look out!" Mia shouted.

But it was already too late. An Angel swiped its extended claws and the man fell to his knees, his face screwed up in silent agony. The Angel retracted its claws and picked him up by his head. He hung limply in its hand, blood pouring from a deep laceration on his back.

"Shit," Mia said, looking away.

Fat Brenda barged past her and screamed abuse at the Angels as she opened fire with her submachine gun. Her huge arms juddered like jelly. Bullets fell in a pile several meters away. Oblivious to it all, the Angel holding the man turned and walked away with its prize, leaving behind a trail of dripping blood. The remaining two Angels split up and walked in separate directions. Then one stopped and turned to look straight at Fat Brenda while she continued firing. Mia could see its mouth opening and closing, but no sound came from it. Two more Angels appeared from somewhere and joined it. The first Angel raised a hand and the others turned to look at Fat Brenda. Then all three shuffled forward, their spindly legs rising high with each step.

"FB, run!" Mia shouted.

But whether Fat Brenda couldn't hear her over the roar of the gun, or she just didn't care, she held her ground and continued firing while the Angels waddled closer. They stopped six feet away from her and just stood there, staring down at her as if they were studying her.

Fat Brenda stopped firing and stared back. "Come on then, you ugly freaks. What are you waiting for? Come and get me."

The Angels pulled blue disks from their chests and held them out. They took a step closer. Then another.

Fat Brenda backed away, her gun still trained on the three Angels. "Yeah, that's right, come out here and get me you bastards." She turned and ran to a burnt-out army truck and dived behind it, her gun's barrel pointing over the crumpled hood.

Mia curled her finger around her own submachine gun's trigger as the Angels stepped closer, the disks still held out before them. They reached the pile of bullets that marked the edge of the force-field and stepped over them. A blue beam shot from one of the disks. The truck Fat Brenda hid behind exploded into flames. Mia jerked back the trigger on the submachine gun.

An Angel squealed as bullets tore through its body and sent yellow fluid spurting from its back. It stumbled and fell. A second Angel dropped down to all fours and made for the burning truck. The third spun to face Mia, its blue disk glowing.

Mia ran for cover behind the tank. She collided with Wicked Tina and they both tumbled down together. The Angel's shot went wide and the laser beam whizzed over their heads. Margot aimed and fired back, but a split second before she pulled the trigger the Angel dropped down to all fours and the hail of bullets flew harmlessly over it. It galloped forward, making straight for Margot.

Margot turned to run, but stumbled and fell. She just had enough time to roll onto her back and raise her gun when the Angel pounced onto her. It batted the gun from her hand with a single swipe, then reared up with the claws of one hand extended to slash down at her face.

Mia scrabbled to her knees and raised the gun to shoot it, but before she could fire Wicked Tina pulled the dagger from her boot and ran at the Angel. She raised it above her head and plunged it into the Angel's back with a roar of hatred. The blade pierced its outer shell with a sickening crunch. Yellow fluid spurted into Wicked Tina's face. The Angel screeched and flailed its arms. Wicked Tina used both hands to tear the dagger down its body. The Angel reared up, staggered back, then spun around several times with its arms outstretched. Wicked Tina lost her grip and fell, the dagger still embedded in the Angel's back. She just had enough time to roll out of the way as the Angel swiped down at her with its claws.

Mia aimed at the Angel's head as it reared up again for another swipe.

"Stay down!" Mia shouted to Wicked Tina.

The Angel turned to Mia and dropped to all fours, then darted forward. Mia aimed lower as it sped toward her, and screamed in defiance as she pulled the trigger. The Angel's body juddered as it ran, yellow fluid spurting in all directions. Mia kept firing in one continuous burst, her arms aching from the vibration. The Angel stumbled and fell three feet from her and rolled to one side. It reached toward her with one hand. The blue disk clasped between its fingers began to glow.

Then its body juddered and it lay still. Mia stared at the disk, unable to move. She expected it to fire at any second and incinerate her instantly at such close range. But instead, the glow diminished and the disk returned to its normal dull blue colour. She closed her eyes and exhaled, realising she had been holding her breath the entire time.

Then she remembered Fat Brenda. She sprang to her feet and turned to the burning truck. "FB, you okay?" she shouted. "FB?"

Fat Brenda stepped out from behind the truck and walked over to her, a wide grin on her face. "Piece of piss, this killing Angels lark," she said. "The useless bastards just stand there and let you blow them away. Let's see if we can get some more to come out."

"Or we could just stroll in there and get *them*," Wicked Tina said. She held up one of the blue disks. Yellow goo dripped from the remains of three Angel fingers still attached to it.

20

Wicked Tina strode up to the pile of bullets marking the perimeter of the force-field around the Angel compound, then paused and glanced at Mia.

"Well go on then," Fat Brenda said. "It's your idea, so let's see if it works."

Wicked Tina nodded, then reached out tentatively with one hand. "It's gone soft," she said. "All rubbery, like a balloon. And it's warm, too."

"But can you get through it?" Fat Brenda's voice had a hint of impatience behind it.

"I'll try." She stepped forward, her hand outstretched. "Yeah, it looks like it. I think I might be—"

Wicked Tina's voice cut off mid-word. She turned around, her face screwed up in disgust. Her mouth moved, but no sound came from it. She swung back her arm and tossed the disk to Mia. It seemed to visibly slow in mid-air, and Mia caught it in both hands and stepped forward with it. Wicked Tina was right, the barrier felt soft and pliable. Mia probed it with her fingers while she held the disk in her other hand. She felt a slight resistance as she pushed harder, then something gave way and peeled back down to her wrist. She drew in a breath and held it, then took a step closer to Wicked Tina. The invisible rubbery barrier stretched over her body for a second, then seemed to burst around her and she was through.

The stench of excrement and blood, in stark contrast with the sweet, fresh air on the other side, made her eyes water. She gagged and almost threw up.

"Well I did warn you to be ready for it, honey," Wicked Tina said.

Mia spat, then tossed the disk underarm to Fat Brenda. "We couldn't hear you," she said. "Whatever it is, it seems to cut all the sound off too."

Fat Brenda fumbled for the disk and dropped it. She bent

down to retrieve it, then walked through and tossed it back through for Margot.

"Right then," she said once Margot joined them, "let's find some more Angels to kill."

The four women hurried over to the nearest dome. It felt warm and smooth, its surface flawless. They worked their way around it, over a hundred feet in diameter, keeping an eye out for any Angels as they went. Mia looked for anything resembling a doorway, but found the dome's surface uniform in its lack of features. Just the same flat metallic blue tone all the way around.

"I saw one of the Angels go inside one of these," Mia said, "so there must be some sort of door somewhere. So where the hell is it?"

"Maybe it's them disks that opens them?" Wicked Tina asked.

Mia shrugged. "I don't think so, it was carrying someone at the time and I don't think it used the disk. But I couldn't really see properly, so I guess it could've done."

She took the Angel disk from Margot and held it up to the dome while she walked around it again. Nothing happened.

"I guess we'll have to wait for an Angel to go inside, see how it does it," Margot said.

"Sod that," Fat Brenda said. "I see any of those bastards and I'm killing them straight away."

"No, Margot's right," Mia said, forcing the Angel disk into one of the pockets of her leather jacket. "We need to find out how to get in those domes. At least one of them has got people inside it, remember."

"What, like the people who shot our bikes to bits, then tried to kill us? So what? They can stay there for all I care. I'm here for one reason only, and that's killing Angels. Nothing else matters."

Mia sighed. There was no reasoning with Fat Brenda once she'd made her mind up like that. "Yeah, okay. Fair enough, I get that. But there will be Angels in there too, maybe hundreds of them. Think how much fun that would be, shooting through the doorway, watching them all get blown to bits right in front of you."

Fat Brenda grinned. "Yeah, you might have a point there." She rapped her knuckles on the dome's surface. The sound was hollow and metallic, and rang out like a bell. "Come on out you ugly bastards, it's party time."

Mia tensed. She readied her submachine gun, expecting to see dozens of Angels rushing out to investigate. But nothing happened.

Fat Brenda sighed. "Fine. I guess we wait then."

It was almost an hour before another flying saucer loomed above them. They crouched down in the shadows of one of the domes and watched while it dropped down and hovered above the ground. Then four Angels seemed to just appear from behind one of the domes before plodding over to the spacecraft.

Fat Brenda raised her gun as soon as they came into sight. She grinned as her finger curled over the trigger.

"Not yet," Mia whispered, placing a hand on Fat Brenda's arm and forcing the gun back down. "We need to know how they get in and out of the domes, remember?"

Fat Brenda sighed, but left the gun pointing at the ground.

A young girl, little more than eight years old, fell naked from the ship. Wicked Tina peered through the sight of her sniper rifle as an Angel bent down to pick up the girl and walked over to one of the domes with her. It splayed the fingers of its free hand against the dome's surface and an arched area of the dome shimmered in multiple colours. The Angel walked inside and the shimmering stopped, the dome becoming solid once more.

"Did you see how it did it?" Margot asked.

Wicked Tina, still looking through the sight, raised a thumb and nodded. "I reckon so, honey. There's like three little dents quite high up, you'd need to know they were there to even notice them."

"You think you can find them again?"

"Yeah, I reckon I should be able to."

Two more naked captives were taken into the same dome before the Angel ship left. The women waited until the last of the three Angels returned to the dome they had appeared from, then crept closer to the one they'd seen them take the captives into. Wicked Tina pointed up at the three dents she said the Angel had used to create an opening. Mia found them hard to make out at first, but then she saw them. About six inches apart, in a triangular formation, nine feet from the ground. Too high for any of them to reach, even if they stretched up on their toes.

"Well so much for that idea," Fat Brenda said, staring up at the three dents. "That's four of the bastards I could've killed just then, and now they've gone. Next time I'm blowing them away as soon as I see them."

"No," Mia said, "we need to get in there first, get those children to safety. And the adults too, maybe they can help us fight the Angels. The more of us there are, the better our chances. Tina, you're the tallest, you get on FB's back and see if you can reach them."

Fat Brenda sighed. "This is just a waste of good killing time if you ask me." But she bent over and clutched her knees anyway, so Wicked Tina could climb onto her back.

Wicked Tina steadied herself with the palm of one hand against the dome's surface while she stretched up with the other. Even standing on her toes on Fat Brenda's back she was still over a foot short of reaching the three dents.

"It's no good," she said, "they're too far up."

"Get on my shoulders," Margot said.

Margot stood behind Fat Brenda and braced herself against the dome while Wicked Tina side-stepped across to her and placed a boot on her left shoulder. Mia reached up and helped her get the other foot in place while Fat Brenda moved out of the way. Margot gripped Wicked Tina's boots and inched sideways until she was beneath the three dents in the dome's surface. Wicked Tina reached up once more and splayed the fingers of one hand to place her thumb and middle finger against the bottom two dents. With the other hand she placed her index finger against the top dent.

An area of the dome before them shimmered. Mia reached out a hand to check it was no longer solid, then rushed through with her submachine gun raised. The much stronger stench of human excrement hit her immediately, and the discordant moan of hundreds of tortured souls burned into her eardrums. It was so bright in there she had to look down and shield her eyes until they could adjust to the harsh lighting.

Margot and Wicked Tina bumped into her as they entered the dome together. Fat Brenda swore as she joined them. She gagged as she held both hands over her nose and mouth. Mia squinted around her. Her face paled and her mouth dropped open.

"Holy shit," Wicked Tina said. "What the hell is this?"

Mia didn't have an answer for her. She'd never seen anything like it before.

A long spiral row of naked men, women, boys and girls almost filled the entire dome, crushed up against each other like some kind of nightmarish orgy. Their legs were caked in piss and shit, their arms and upper bodies a mass of septic scabs and scratches. What looked like three white tentacles held them in a standing position, one secured around each wrist and a third disappearing down the throats of their upturned heads. Every now and again this tentacle would pulsate, and their moans of anguish would change to a choking, gagging sound for a couple of seconds before resuming once more. Most of them were morbidly obese, bigger even than Fat Brenda.

The three new arrivals hung together close by. They were rake-thin by comparison, almost anorexic in appearance, their ribs protruding from their skin. All three trembled in fear, making gurgling sounds around the tentacles inserted in their throats. Mia shivered at the thought of ending up hanging there herself. She thought about the wild boy from the woods, and wondered if this was where he had ended up or if he had somehow managed to escape. If this was where Suzy would be right now if Mia hadn't stopped the Angel from taking her back to its ship.

Margot and Wicked Tina gaped at the trussed up bodies before them. Even Fat Brenda seemed affected by what she saw. Her face was white, her eyes wide and staring. Her submachine gun shook as she gripped it tight in both hands. She grimaced, then raised the gun and aimed at the bodies closest to her.

"No!" Mia said, louder than she intended, and stepped in front of Fat Brenda with her hands raised. "For God's sake, we need to help them, not kill them."

Fat Brenda frowned. "You're kidding, right? Look at the state of them, they're suffering. The kindest thing to do is put them out of their misery, and you know it."

"Some of them haven't been here long, we could at least save those. Besides, the others might know something useful, like what the hell is going on here and how we can stop it."

Wicked Tina and Margot stepped closer, their motorcycle

boots splashing in an inch of effluence coating the smooth hard flooring. As they moved away from the dome's inner surface the shimmering ceased and the wall became solid once more. They both spun toward it in alarm.

Mia's heart flipped when she saw their only way out of the dome disappear before her eyes. But then she noticed three dents high up in the surface identical to the ones outside.

"It's okay," she said, pointing at them. "We can open it again once we're done here, we just need to remember where they are."

Wicked Tina nodded and placed a spare sniper rifle bullet on the ground to mark its position.

Mia walked along the spiral row of standing bodies with Wicked Tina, trying not to look at the pleading bloodshot eyes staring down at her from both sides. Bodies jerked as they tried to turn themselves around to see what was going on, and their muffled moans became louder as she passed them by. The further they went toward the centre of the dome, the fatter the people suspended there became. The men had long beards hanging from their double chins, while the women all had huge, sagging breasts. Menstrual blood dribbled down the legs of several of the ones she passed.

"Why are they here?" Wicked Tina asked.

Mia didn't have an answer for that either. None of it made any sense. Why would the Angels keep these people alive after they had put so much effort into wiping the rest of humanity from the face of the earth? Some kind of zoo, an attempt to save their species from extinction? But that would indicate a level of remorse Mia doubted the Angels were even capable of feeling. Maybe they kept them to amuse themselves by torturing them? That would explain all the cuts and scratches on their bodies, but it wouldn't explain why they were all so well fed or why there was so many of them.

Whatever the reason, whatever this was about, in the end it just didn't matter. All that mattered was they were suffering. She had to free them, get them as far away from those domes as she could. The Angel disk in the pocket of her leather jacket would get them through the force-field if they were lucky enough to get that far before another flying saucer showed up, and if they could make it back to the road she could hand out guns from the truck. That would at least give them all a fighting chance to survive when the Angels came looking for them.

Wicked Tina must have read her mind because she slung the sniper rifle over her shoulder, pulled the dagger from her boot, and reached up to hack at the tentacle rammed down a man's throat. Grey, viscous fluid spurted from it as she punctured its surface with a crunching sound. The man's head slumped down to his chest once she had carved all the way through. Then Wicked Tina gripped one of the tentacles securing his wrists and slid the dagger's blade across it. As soon as it severed, his arm flopped down limp by his side. Wicked Tina sliced through the other tentacle and he fell to his knees before keeling over and splashing down face-first into the huge puddle of piss and liquid shit by his feet.

Mia crouched next to him and rolled him onto his back as he choked on the effluence he lay in. She thought about putting her submachine gun down so she would have both hands free to help him, then thought better of it and stuffed it barrel-first inside her leather jacket instead. Supporting the man's head with one hand, she gripped the short length of tentacle projecting from his mouth and tried to pull it out.

It was stuck tight.

The man stared up at her as she lowered the back of his head into the spilt bodily fluids once more and placed a hand on his forehead to hold it down. With her other hand she squeezed the tentacle tight and tugged. The end disappearing down his throat was ridged, and she had to jerk it out inch by inch while the man gagged and convulsed beneath her. It was almost an extra foot long before it finally came free, long enough to reach right into his stomach. He shuddered and coughed, then a fountain of grey vomit erupted from his mouth and he choked once more.

Mia tilted his head to one side until he stopped vomiting and just lay there dry-heaving.

"It'll be okay," she said, "we're going to get you out of here."

The man tried to sit up, but couldn't manage it. He locked eyes with Mia and seemed to be trying to say something, but all he could manage was a rasping sound.

"Jesus Christ," Margot yelled from near the centre of the dome. "You need to get over here, quick."

"Yeah, give us a second, honey."

Wicked Tina was busy cutting another man free, her blade

already half-way through the tentacle inserted in his mouth.

"No, you need to come right now. All of you. There's something you need to see."

Wicked Tina lowered her dagger, told the man she would come back later, then made her way down the narrow spiral gap between the bodies to where Margot's voice had come from.

"Holy shit," she exclaimed a few seconds later. "How is that even possible?"

"What is it?" Mia asked, still crouched beside the man lying on the ground. He'd started blubbering, tears streaming from his eyes, his entire flabby body wobbling with each sob. But at least he'd stopped spewing, so he wouldn't choke if she left him alone for a short while to see what Margot and Wicked Tina had found.

"You'd better come and see this for yourself, honey. You're going to freak when you do."

"I'll come back, I promise," Mia said to the man by her feet.

He whimpered when she rose up and turned away from him.

Mia made her way between the rows of flesh to where Margot and Wicked Tina stood staring at one of the bodies standing there.

"What is it?" she asked once more. "What have you found?"

Wicked Tina stepped back and gestured, a thin smile on her lips. "Take a look for yourself, honey."

Mia stared at the man's tattooed chest and gasped. Even with all the cuts and scratches, and the extra hundred and fifty pounds of flab stretching it out of shape, there was no mistaking that image.

The grim reaper riding a motorcycle.

Her mouth dropped open as she looked up for confirmation.

Bonehead's pallid face stared down at her. A severed tentacle dangled from his mouth like an elephant's trunk, grey mush dripping from the end of it.

"Get him down!" Mia screamed.

Wicked Tina reached up and cut through the tentacles securing his wrists while Mia held him upright. In his new bloated form Bonehead was too big to get her arms all the way around his waist, so she gripped him by the sides instead, her fingers disappearing into his flesh.

Bonehead's knees gave out as soon as he was released and he slumped down, taking Mia with him. She held his face in her hands and stared into it, shaking her head slowly, amazed he was still alive. How was it even possible? Had he been there all this time, just hanging there?

Heavy footsteps splashed closer. Fat Brenda gaped down at Bonehead.

"What the hell? Is Dirk here too?"

She wheeled around, staring at the faces of the other bodies suspended nearby.

"Dirk! Where are you?" she shouted, running back down the spiral. "Dirk!"

Mia held Bonehead's head still while Margot gripped the feeding tentacle in both hands and stretched it out. "This is going to hurt," she said, "so brace yourself."

Bonehead nodded once and clenched his fists. His long, jagged fingernails dug into the palm of his hands and blood dripped from them. His eyes bulged and his body spasmed when Margot tugged on the tentacle. Mia held him tight as he struggled against her. Then he let out a muffled, anguished cry and grabbed the tentacle and yanked it from Margot, catching her off guard and causing her to stumble forward.

"You've got to let us pull it out," Mia said, "it's the only way."

Bonehead grabbed the tentacle and squeezed it so tight his knuckles turned white and more blood dripped from his wrists. His flabby biceps bulged, and with a quick jerk and a muffled scream of pure rage he yanked the ridged tentacle another six inches from of his mouth. He paused, tears streaming down his cheeks, breathing quickly through his nose, then screamed again as he pulled it out fully and threw it away in disgust.

"Mia," he said in a faint croak. Blood and bile dripped down his chin.

Mia placed a finger over Bonehead's cracked lips. "Don't try to talk."

Then the words just babbled out of her. She had so much to tell him, and she still couldn't believe he was really still alive, that it wasn't just another messed up dream.

"We're going to get you out of here, there's someone I want you to meet, I called him Little Bonehead because he looks just like you, and you're going to love him just as much as I do, there's a place we can all live together, I think it's going to be safe there, we lost our bikes but we can get some new ones and start again, we'll teach Little Bonehead how to ride, find him some little tiny leathers and a helmet so he won't get hurt if he falls off, he's in Northumberland somewhere, with the Brownies, there was these soldiers too, but—"

"Mia," Bonehead rasped. He grimaced as he tried to swallow. "Mia ... there's ... something I need to ... tell you before I wake up."

"You are awake, Bonehead. This is really happening. We're getting out of here, you'll see."

"I ... know. That's what you ... always say ... and ... I believe you ... but before you go ..."

"I'm not going anywhere without you, I promise."

"... before you go ... I need you to know how ... how I feel about you. I want you to ... live your life where ... wherever you are right now ... knowing you were more than ... just a mama to me."

Bonehead closed his eyes and his head went limp in Mia's arms. She watched his chest rise and fall rhythmically and smiled. It filled her heart with joy to know he felt the same way about her as she did about him. She'd let him rest for as long as it took, then get him to the jeep, take him back to Northumberland where they could spend the rest of their lives together.

She was still smiling when a shadow fell over her.

She looked up. Fat Brenda stared down at her with a scowl on her face.

"All very touching, I'm sure. But I need to know what happened back at the camp that day. How is he still alive, when the others aren't?"

Without warning, Fat Brenda kicked Bonehead in the ribs. Bonehead's eyes shot open and he cried out in pain.

"You hear me, you bald bastard?" Fat Brenda screamed down at him. "What did you do, did you make a deal with the Angels? Your life for theirs, is that it?" She aimed her submachine gun at Bonehead's chest. "You'd better start talking, right now."

But before Bonehead could reply, a woman's frantic scream echoed around the dome.

Along with the chirp of an Angel.

21

Fat Brenda spun toward the scream, her gun still raised. She stepped forward and barged her way between two naked men suspended before her.

"Don't shoot," Mia called after her as loud as she dared. "We don't want them to know we're in here."

"Sod that," Fat Brenda said. "We're here to kill the bastards, remember?"

Mia swore. She eased her arm from under Bonehead and lay him down flat in the pool of liquid excrement. "Wait here," she said, standing up. She took the submachine gun from her leather jacket and followed Fat Brenda through the rows of naked bodies, desperate to stop her from wrecking everything.

Through small gaps between the standing figures she could see an Angel holding a naked woman at arm's length. Its fingers were curled around the top of her head and her arms and legs thrashed as she continued screaming, desperate to free herself from its clutches. The Angel reached out for one of the vacant tentacles and looped it around her left wrist. It seemed to contract around it and raise her arm above her head all by itself while the Angel turned its attention to her right wrist. Then it tilted her head up and forced a third tentacle down her throat. The woman's scream turned into a choking gurgle.

Fat Brenda opened fire and the dome filled with a deafening roar. Men, women and children standing in her path jerked as bullets tore through them, sending blood spurting like party streamers in all directions. The Angel chirped and its long fingers shot to the blue disk attached to its chest. Fat Brenda roared and ran at the Angel like a woman possessed, her gun spitting out round after round as she went. Bullets thudded into the Angel's body, making it stumble back against the wall of the dome. Some ricocheted off the Angel's disk with a metallic ping, but most hit their target and reduced its body to a yellow pulp. She continued firing as it slid down the inside of the dome, leaving a yellow smear. Its eye exploded with a wet squelch, then bullets were flying everywhere as they bounced off the curved wall behind it.

"Stop shooting!" Mia shouted, ducking low as one of the men standing beside her was hit in the face by a stray bullet.

Fat Brenda continued firing for another three seconds, then turned around, smiling. "Now that," she said, "was—"

An area of the dome's surface shimmered and another Angel stepped through it holding a naked man. It looked at the remains of the first Angel splattered against the wall, emitted a series of loud chirping sounds, then dropped the man and reached for its disk.

"Look out!" Mia shouted.

Fat Brenda spun, raising the gun once more. She pulled the trigger but nothing happened. She looked down at it, swore, then tried again. Still nothing. The Angel pointed its disk at Fat Brenda. Fat Brenda backed away while she pulled off the gun's clip. She dropped it and reached into her leather jacket for a fresh one.

Mia knew Fat Brenda wouldn't have time to reload. She rushed forward, slipping the safety catch on her own gun as two more Angels stepped through the shimmering opening.

Wicked Tina's rifle boomed, and an Angel's eye disintegrated, taking off the top of its head as the high-calibre bullet burst through the other side. Then Margot was by her side, spraying more bullets into the remaining two Angels. The naked man just had enough time to roll out of the way and save himself as the Angels toppled over emitting a piercing shrill squeal.

Margot ran to the shimmering arch in the dome's surface. An Angel lay there half in, half out, yellow fluid pumping from its ruined body. Its long fingers twitched as Margot jumped over it and disappeared. She returned a second later, grabbed the naked man by the arm and hauled him to his feet.

"They're coming!" she yelled as she ran for cover, dragging the man along with her.

He stared, wide-eyed, at the rows and rows of naked flesh before him. Some writhed in agony from bullet wounds, others hung limp and bloody, already dead.

"What is this place?" he asked.

"No time to explain," Margot said from her position behind

one of the corpses. "But you'd better get out of the way if you don't want to get caught in the crossfire."

The man gaped at her, then did as he was told and squeezed through the rows of bodies. Mia headed him off and told him to make for the centre of the dome and stay there. She stepped forward, her gun trained on the shimmering doorway.

Then dozens of Angels swarmed inside on all fours. Mia opened fire a split second after Margot and Fat Brenda. Angels shuddered and fell, but for every one they killed two more took their place. Mia's gun grew hot as the Angel bodies piled up around the entrance. Her arms ached from the constant vibration, but she had to keep firing at the fresh wave of Angels clambering over their fallen comrades. She knew if even just one of them got through it would rip them all to pieces.

A blinding blue flash filled the dome. Mia ducked instinctively and turned her back as an energy beam shot toward her, incinerating everything in its path, Angels included. The blast wave knocked her off her feet and she splashed down face-first, the gun clattering away from her as more blue lasers zipped overhead. An intense heat scorched her back, then her hair caught fire. She rolled over, ignoring the taste of human shit in her mouth, and doused the flames on the back of her head. She sat up and spat, then scrabbled around for her fallen gun as three more Angels galloped into the dome.

Wicked Tina's sniper rifle blasted and an Angel flew backwards with a gaping hole in its head. Another turned toward her, then it too fell with a second shot to the head. Mia found her gun and raised it. Excrement dripped from it as she aimed at the remaining Angel and pulled the trigger, spraying it with a short burst of bullets. It toppled over with a squeal and thrashed its arms and legs trying to right itself. Mia ran over and pointed the gun down at its head and pulled the trigger. Yellow goo splattered up into her face.

Then she remembered the Angel's laser beam and its trail of destruction.

"Bonehead!" she yelled, running back through the trench of charred and smouldering bodies. It had all happened so quick she hadn't had time to think about anything other than her own survival, but now the thought of what might have happened to Bonehead filled her with dread. She couldn't lose him again, not now. She'd only just found him again.

Fat Brenda sat on the ground rubbing the back of her head. She must have been knocked over by the blast too, but she seemed okay. No sign of Margot anywhere, but Mia didn't have time to think about that as she ran back to where she had left Bonehead. She looked left and right. Blackened bodies hung either side of her, the white tentacles holding them upright seemingly untouched by the devastation. She headed right, using the barrel of her gun to part the bodies just enough to squeeze between them. Bonehead sat upright several rows down, rubbing his legs. The man Margot had dragged into the dome stood beside him with his hands covering his genitals. He looked embarrassed about his nakedness as Mia approached.

"Bonehead, are you okay?"

"Yeah. Did you get them all?"

"Yeah, I think so. Can you walk yet?"

Bonehead shrugged. "I'll give it a try, but you'll need to help me up."

Mia held out her hand and Bonehead grasped it. She tugged, but Bonehead just rocked forward, his new bloated form far too heavy for her to lift.

"Don't just stand there, help me," Mia said to the other man.

"His name's Tom," Bonehead said. "He's from Whitehaven, somewhere in Cumberland, apparently, but I've never heard of it. Used to work at Windscale Nuclear Power Plant, he's like some sort of scientist or something."

Tom stepped forward and nodded, then helped Mia haul Bonehead to his feet. With an arm around each of their shoulders they walked him through the rows of suspended bodies. Mia avoided looking into the eyes of the ones still alive. She felt bad about leaving them behind to suffer, but knew there was little she could do to help. Bonehead had to be her priority now. She had to get him somewhere safe before more Angels came.

At the shimmering doorway, Wicked Tina popped her head out. It looked freaky, like her head had just vanished from her shoulders.

"Seems to be clear out there," she said, her head reappearing once more. "I reckon we should make a run for it now, while we can."

"I'm out of ammo," Margot said, walking toward her empty-handed. "You still got that disk thing?"

"I think Mia had it last, but there's plenty more lying around we could use instead." She slung the rifle over one shoulder and took out her dagger.

As Mia, Bonehead and Tom got closer, Fat Brenda stamped up to them. "You ready to tell me what happened yet?" she said to Bonehead.

"For God's sake, FB," Mia said, "can't it wait until later? We don't have time for shit like this."

"No, it's okay," Bonehead said, "she should know what happened."

"You're damn right I should."

"Well let's at least keep walking," Mia said. "The sooner we get out of here the better."

"We was all tripping on mushrooms," Bonehead said. "Basher had this idea that if we stretched really tall we could touch the sky and put all the stars out one by one. So that's what we do, we all stand there reaching up, trying to put the stars out. Then Tanner, I think it was, he says stars are made out of fire, so we would just burn our fingers on them, and what we really needed to do was chuck some water up at them instead. So a few of us goes over to the lake to get some water, but then we realise we haven't got nothing to put it in. So I go to me tent to see if I can find something, don't I? Only I can't find nothing, but then I get this idea, yeah? So I take me boots off, thinking if we fill them with water and chuck them up at the sky that should do the trick. But while I'm doing that, there's this like humming sound everywhere."

"Angels," Mia said.

"Well yeah, I know that now, but at the time I thought it was this giant wasp, yeah? Like Superwasp or something, coming to get me and stab me in the face with its massive arse dagger. Well you know I don't like wasps, right?"

"If you're going to tell me you hid in your tent while everyone else got killed because you're scared of wasps I'm going to shoot you right now," Fat Brenda said.

"No I didn't, honest. Anyway, everyone's shouting by then, and I reckon this Superwasp must be attacking them or something, so I grab me shotgun and run out so I can shoot it.

Only I haven't got no boots on 'cause I took them off didn't I, and the grass is a bit wet, so I go flying and bang me head on something. The next thing I know I'm strapped on this like table type thing stark bollock naked and there's all these Angels poking me, and I can hear Deano shouting at them somewhere nearby."

"Wait, you mean Deano's here?" Margot asked, spinning around.

"Yeah. Well, he was. But he, um..."

"Well is he here or not?"

"What about Dirk?" Fat Brenda demanded. "Is he here too?"

"No, it were just me and Deano what got fetched here. I didn't see Dirk. Maybe he got away before they took us, I don't know."

"What about Deano?" Margot stood in front of Bonehead and blocked their progress. "Where is he now?"

"He, um ... well, it was when they dropped us down when we got here. They dropped me first, then this Angel grabs me head and lifts me up. Deano, he ... well, he tries to leg it, doesn't he? He's quicker than me, good at running and stuff. Only the Angels are quicker, yeah? And there was loads of them all chasing after him. Anyway, he's um ... well ... shit, they got him, okay? Sorry."

"Is he still alive?" Margot stared into Bonehead's eyes.

Bonehead looked down and shook his head. "Sorry Margot, there was nothing I could do, honest."

"No!" Margot yelled. She turned and punched one of the corpses hanging nearby. Continued punching it with both fists until Fat Brenda wrapped her arms around her from behind and pulled her away.

Tears streamed down Margot's face. "Give me your gun," she said to Mia.

"What do you want it for?" Mia asked.

Margot shook off Fat Brenda and made a grab for the gun. Mia tried to hide it behind her back, but Margot was too quick for her. She held onto its grip while Margot tugged the clip and barrel with both hands.

"Just give me the damn gun," Margot said, and wrenched it out of Mia's hand.

"Don't do anything stupid," Mia said.

Margot gave out a short laugh. "A bit late for that, don't

you think? Come on, let's go. There's nothing here for us now."

Wicked Tina handed Fat Brenda and Margot an Angel disk each, then they both stepped out of the dome together brandishing their submachine guns. Wicked Tina pulled the sniper rifle from her shoulder and followed, while Mia and Tom helped Bonehead to the exit. By the time they got there, the others were already running across the clearing between the domes.

"Wait for us," Mia shouted, but they continued running.

Then she glanced up and saw an Angel ship approaching from the west at high speed.

22

"Angels!" Mia yelled. Wicked Tina froze and spun toward her. Mia pointed. "Over there, coming in fast."

Wicked Tina looked up, then ran to the nearest dome and disappeared behind it. Mia rushed Bonehead along, desperate to join her before the Angels arrived and saw them. But then Bonehead stumbled and fell to his knees, pulling Mia and Tom over with him. Tom bolted, leaving Mia cursing after him while she tried to get Bonehead back onto his feet by herself.

The flying saucer loomed overhead, then dropped down to hover between the domes at a height of ten feet from the ground. Margot and Fat Brenda fired up at it with a continuous burst, then lowered their aim as dozens of Angels dropped from it. Some were hit and spun through the air before they fell dead on the ground. Others galloped forward on all fours, heading straight for the two women while more and more Angels fell from the ship. Fat Brenda turned and ran.

Margot stood her ground, screaming abuse at the Angels while she continued firing and their bodies piled up before her. The remaining Angels split into two groups to dodge around them. Margot waved her gun between both factions as they closed in on her. Then an Angel pounced, its front claws extended. Margot tilted the gun up and shot it in the face as it flew toward her, but the Angel's limp body struck her in the chest and knocked her onto her back. Two more Angels pounced simultaneously. Margot screamed in agony as their claws slashed at her.

Mia turned away with a sob when she saw blood spurting and heard the sound of Margot's flesh being torn apart. She felt like screaming herself, but she knew that would only draw the Angels' attention to her and Bonehead. She tried not to listen to the ripping sounds that continued behind her for long seconds. Another good friend gone, and nothing she could have done to stop it. She swore to herself Margot would be the last, and rubbed the tears away angrily. She had to shut it all out, there would be time for grieving later.

With a strength and determination she never knew she was capable of, Mia managed to get Bonehead back onto his feet and dragged him back inside the dome. They crunched over the limbs of fallen Angels and made their way between the rows of suspended men and women.

Once she thought she had gone far enough, Mia squeezed Bonehead between two of the bodies and told him to stay there while she headed further into the dome. She took the Angel disk from her pocket and placed it on the ground, then covered it up with a mound of sloppy excrement and studied the faces of the men and women hanging nearby as they stared down at her. If this worked, she would need to remember where the disk was when she needed it. She walked further, then crouched down next to one of the burnt corpses and unzipped her boots. She pulled them off, then stuffed her socks inside them before peeling off the rest of her clothes. She lay her leather jacket down on top of the boots with the lining facing up and placed the rest of her clothes on that, then made her way back to Bonehead naked.

She had only just reached him when two more Angels entered the dome. They chirped together while they inspected the bloody corpses of the men and women who had been caught by Fat Brenda's frenzied shooting, completely ignoring the remains of the dozens of Angels they had killed. One of them reached out and prodded a woman's body with a single finger. It chirped again, then retracted a claw and cut through the tentacles holding her upright. The other Angel picked her up by her head and waddled back out of the dome with her. Seconds later eight more Angels entered the dome and began removing more human corpses.

Mia could feel Bonehead's knees weakening, and tightened her grip around him to hold him upright. His face was buried between the huge breasts of an obese woman and she worried he might suffocate if he stayed there too long. An Angel walked upright toward her, studying the rows of burnt and blackened bodies standing close by. It chirped, and three more Angels joined it. Mia hoped they wouldn't look too closely at the surrounding bodies while they removed the charred corpses. If they were caught now they would spend the rest of their lives hanging from tentacles, being force-fed a diet of grey slop. Mia would rather die fighting than suffer a fate like that.

Above the chirping of the Angels and the sound of bodies splashing down to the ground when they were freed from their tentacles, Mia heard shouts coming from the direction of the shimmering opening. She tilted her head to listen better, but couldn't make out who it was. Then Wicked Tina's hysterical voice roared out.

"Get off me you freak! I'm going to kill you all, you hear me?" She continued with a tirade of abuse, her voice growing louder by the second. Mia heard a ripping sound, then a faint splash. "You know what I'm going to do to you? I'm going to tear your filthy head off, you ugly bastard! Then I'm going to—"

Wicked Tina gagged and made a choking gurgle sound.

A tear rolled down Mia's cheek. They'd got Wicked Tina and strung her up, and there was nothing she could do about it. Even if her and Bonehead lived through this, there would be no way of freeing her without something to cut through those tentacles, and the Angels would have taken Wicked Tina's dagger along with her rifle when they caught her.

It seemed like hours before the last of the Angels finally left the dome, but Mia had no way of knowing for sure. It could have just been a matter of minutes for all she knew. She relaxed and gave out a long sigh before easing herself and Bonehead out from between the mounds of flesh either side of them.

"You okay?" she asked, hands on Bonehead's shoulders.

Bonehead nodded. "Yeah." He turned and limped forward, reaching out and clutching the shoulders of men and women around him to steady himself. "I don't reckon I'll be running any marathons for a while, but I can make me way out of here just fine."

Mia retrieved her clothes and shuffled into them, then searched for the faces that marked where she had hidden the Angel disk. She found it and scooped it up, wiped as much shit from it as she could on her jeans, then placed it in the pocket of her leather jacket before following Bonehead to the dome's still shimmering exit. They were lucky there was still an Angel corpse lying there, because it would have been impossible to open that portal otherwise. Bonehead wouldn't be strong enough to support her weight on his shoulders, and there was no way she'd be able to lift his massive bulk herself.

Bonehead paused before Wicked Tina and tried to prise the tentacles from her wrists. Her clothes lay in rags around her, trodden into the effluence. Blood dripped from a large gash on one side of her face. Her small breasts were bloody too, dozens of scratches covering her chest. Her head jerked as she moaned around the tentacle rammed down her throat.

"We'll come back for you," Mia said. "I promise."

Wicked Tina thrashed and moaned, like she was trying to say something. Bonehead held her upturned face in his hands and nodded. He placed a hand on her chest and gripped the tentacle trailing out of her mouth.

"You ready?" he said.

Wicked Tina clenched a fist and stuck out a thumb. Mia watched her muscles tense. Bonehead jerked the tentacle out inch by inch while Wicked Tina gagged. Then it came free and grey fluid shot from her mouth. She turned her head to one side and spat.

"Don't leave me like this," she croaked.

"We have to," Mia said. "But we'll be back as soon as we can."

Wicked Tina shook her head. "We both know that won't happen." She looked at Bonehead. "I'm ready, honey."

"Ready for what?" Mia asked.

Bonehead stretched up and kissed Wicked Tina on the mouth. "I'll never forget you," he said, then gripped her around the neck and squeezed. Wicked Tina's eyes bulged, but she didn't struggle. She seemed to want it.

"No!" Mia shouted, stepping back. "Bonehead, what the hell are you doing?"

"It's the only way," Bonehead said. "You don't know what it's like in here. I can't let her go through that."

Tears streamed down Mia's face. Bonehead was right, it would be the kindest thing to do. Even if they were lucky enough get away they would never be able to return to save her. But she couldn't watch another friend die, she just couldn't.

Mia turned away with a sob and headed for the shimmering doorway. Then paused. There was something hard beneath her boot. She peered down at the murky effluence and kicked at it with her toe, wondering what it might be. Then she realised what it was and bent down to pick it up.

"Bonehead, stop!" she yelled. "We don't need to do that, we can cut her down."

Bonehead released his grip on Wicked Tina's neck instantly and spun around to face her. "You what?"

"Look!" Mia showed him Wicked Tina's dagger.

Bonehead looped his arms around Wicked Tina's waist and held her tight while Mia hacked through the tentacles securing her wrists. They tore loose, and Wicked Tina slumped down. Bonehead held her upright until she could regain her footing, then released her. Mia frowned at the wounds on the side of her face and down her chest.

"We need to get them cleaned up."

"Later," Wicked Tina said. She rubbed her neck, then glanced around her and pointed. "Get him down as well, I'm not leaving without him."

Mia followed her gaze and saw the scientist, Tom, suspended close by. They cut him down, and Wicked Tina pulled the tentacle from his throat while Bonehead held him still. Mia dragged him to his feet.

"You three get out of here while you can," Tom said, his voice rasping. "I'll free the others."

"What?" Wicked Tina stared at him. "No, you're coming with us. You have to."

Tom shook his head slowly. "I can't just leave them like that. This is something I need to do."

"Are you sure?" Mia asked.

"Yeah, just go. I can handle this, don't worry about me."

Mia nodded and gave him Wicked Tina's dagger, then took the Angel disk from her leather jacket and showed it to him. "There's like an invisible barrier around the domes, these are what get you in and out of it, so grab a few before you leave. Once you're done here, walk straight ahead until you reach it, then hold the disk out and walk through. Good luck."

"You too," Tom said.

Wicked Tina hugged him. "You sure you won't come with us?"

Tom hugged her back. "Maybe I'll see you on the other side?"

"You'd better, honey."

They held the embrace for almost a minute, then Wicked

Tina broke it and turned away. She was crying as she stepped over the Angel corpse and through the portal. Her head reappeared a second later, told them the coast was clear, and Mia and Bonehead joined her out there.

It was pitch black outside, and Mia couldn't see a thing after getting used to the harsh glare inside the dome. She scanned the sky for any signs of Angel ships, but all she saw was stars twinkling down at her. Everything was quiet and still. She noticed for the first time there wasn't even any insects inside the Angels' compound.

"We should stay close, so we don't get lost," she said.

They held hands, with Bonehead in the middle, and walked in a straight line away from the dome they had left Tom in. Mia stared ahead, just about able to make out the outline of the other domes in the pitch darkness surrounding her. She could hear Bonehead's laboured breath to her right, and felt his body brush against her as they paced together slowly.

By the time they reached the force-field surrounding the complex Mia's eyes had started to adjust to the darkness and she could make out the outlines of the wrecked army vehicles beyond. She turned to Bonehead and explained what they had to do. Bonehead nodded and clutched Mia around the waist, drawing her close. Wicked Tina grasped her from the opposite side and the three walked together, matching step with each other. Mia took out the Angel disk and held it up as she approached where she estimated the barrier would be. Its rubbery form wrapped around them, then they burst through into a bitterly cold side-wind.

"Jesus!" Bonehead said, his teeth chattering. "Why is it so cold all of a sudden?" Goosebumps erupted all over his body.

"I don't know," Mia said. She wanted to give Bonehead her leather jacket to keep him warm, but it would be far too small for him so instead she just rubbed his back and held him close.

"You reckon Tom will be okay in there?" Wicked asked, glancing back at the domes.

Mia shrugged. "I don't know. Depends if the Angels wake up or not, assuming they even sleep. There'll be other patrols out there too," she added, gesturing up at the sky. "One of those could come back at any time."

"He saved my life, you know? I kind of owe him for that."

"I'm sure he'll be fine," Mia said. "It's a pretty brave thing he's doing back there." She smiled. "For a *citizen*, anyway."

Wicked Tina laughed. "Yeah. Maybe citizens aren't so bad after all. Who would've thought?"

"So what do we do now?" Bonehead asked.

Mia got her bearings and pointed. "There's a jeep over that hill. Once we get there we can— Oh shit!"

"What's up, honey?" Wicked Tina asked.

"FB's got the keys!" Mia looked back at the domes. "Did you see what happened to her?"

Wicked Tina shrugged and shook her head. "Maybe she got away?"

Mia nodded. "Yeah, let's hope so. And let's hope she hasn't just drove off and left us."

"She wouldn't do that," Bonehead said. "She's one of us, and we take care of our own. She'd never leave a Satan's Bastard in trouble."

"She's changed since you've ... been away," Mia said. "Nothing she does now would surprise me."

The hill was heavy going for Bonehead in his unfit state, and he had to rest every few minutes, so it took almost an hour to reach the stone at the summit. By the time they descended down the other side he was exhausted and Mia and Wicked Tina both had to support him the rest of the way. The jeep with its machinegun turret and the troop transport truck were on the road where they had left them, but there was no sign of Fat Brenda anywhere.

"Shit, now what?" Mia said.

"I can start the jeep," Bonehead said. "Tanner taught me how to hotwire a car years ago, it's piss easy."

"Can you start the truck too?" Wicked Tina asked.

Bonehead shrugged. "Dunno. Probably, yeah, unless it's different. Why?"

"There's loads of guns and stuff inside, it'd be a shame to lose them all, and we might need them one day."

"I'll need a torch and a screwdriver. And a hammer too if you've got one."

Wicked Tina opened up the back of the truck and climbed inside. She returned with a torch, one of the rifles, and a small knife.

"Can't find any tools, will these do?"

Bonehead nodded. "Yeah, should do." He took the rifle and

knife and opened the truck's cab door. "Hold the torch for me so I can see what I'm doing."

Wicked Tina shone the torch inside the truck while Bonehead used the rifle's wooden stock to smash off a plastic panel covering the steering column. He used the knife to prise out a small rectangular junction box, then pulled out one of the wires.

"Usually I'd use a spare bit of wire instead, but this one will do just as well." He grinned. "I'm guessing you won't be needing to use the horn any time soon?"

Wrapping the wire around his knuckles, Bonehead ripped the other end free from where it disappeared under the dashboard and pushed both ends into the junction box. There was a click, and a green light illuminated on the dashboard.

"Is that it?" Wicked Tina asked. "As easy as that?"

"Just one more step, then we're ready to go."

Bonehead stepped down from the cab and opened up the truck's bonnet. Wicked Tina followed him and shone the torch at the engine.

"Now watch this," Bonehead said. He held the knife's blade across two contacts on the left hand side. There was a spark, then the engine rumbled into life. He slammed down the bonnet and turned to Wicked Tina. "Told you it was a piece of piss, didn't I?"

Wicked Tina nodded and clapped him on the shoulder. She handed the torch to Mia, climbed into the cab, and revved the truck's engine before bumping off the road to turn it around. Mia held the torch while Bonehead started up the jeep in a similar way, then climbed into the passenger seat beside him. Bonehead did a quick three-point turn, and the jeep rumbled down the road.

Mia couldn't believe they were finally getting away from there. She thought about Little Bonehead and the girls back in Northumberland and couldn't wait to see them again. They would need to stop off in one of the corpse-strewn towns on the way to see to Wicked Tina's wounds and get some fresh clothes for her and Bonehead so they wouldn't freeze to death, but if they drove all night and didn't stop for long maybe they could make it there by morning.

Mia wound down the window and reached out to adjust the wing mirror so she could see Wicked Tina following behind in the truck. Except she wasn't. She just sat there watching them go, her hands gripping the steering wheel.

"What's she waiting for?"

Bonehead glanced at Mia. "Huh?"

"We need to go back, I think there's something wrong. Maybe her engine stalled or something and she can't get it going again."

Bonehead pulled the jeep over and turned it around. As they approached, Wicked Tina drove off the road and down the embankment.

"What the hell's she doing?" Bonehead asked.

The truck roared up the hill in first gear.

"Shit," Mia said. "Get after her before she does something stupid."

23

Bonehead swung off the road in pursuit of the truck. The jeep bumped down the embankment and jerked Mia forward in her seat. She raised her hands and braced herself against the dashboard as the vehicle began its slow ascent up the hill while the truck disappeared behind the large rock at the hill's summit.

"You need to go faster!"

"I can't," Bonehead said. "This is as fast as it'll go in first gear, and we'd never make it up there in second."

The jeep's engine screamed in protest. Mia could feel the whole vehicle vibrating beneath her. A rattling sound came from somewhere under the bonnet and she hoped it wasn't anything serious. If she'd ever heard anything like that coming from her bike's engine she would've stopped straight away to investigate, but they didn't have that luxury now. They had to keep going and hope for the best, hope the jeep didn't give out on them. Whatever Wicked Tina was up to it could only mean trouble. They had to stop her before she got herself killed.

Bonehead veered right to avoid the rock at the top of the hill and the jeep lurched over to one side, forcing Mia against the door. Then the jeep pointed down as it began its bumpy descent and she was thrown forward into the dashboard once more.

Wicked Tina had already made it down into the valley. The truck's huge wheels ground human bones into the grassland as she weaved around wreckage at speed. Mia watched her slam into the remains of a smaller vehicle and send it spinning out of the way with a wrench of tortured metal.

Bonehead drove slowly with his foot on the brake. Mia pleaded with him to go faster, but he refused to take the risk of losing control.

Wicked Tina parked the truck close to the remains of the tank where they had killed the three Angels and jumped out of the cab. She hurried over to one of the Angel corpses and dragged it over to the truck, then hefted it onto the bonnet.

"Tina, wait!" Mia shouted through the side window.

Wicked Tina glanced at her for a second, then climbed into the truck and shot forward once more. Bonehead pulled up beside the tank and put the jeep into neutral, leaving the engine running. Wicked Tina drove silently between the Angel domes inside the force-field. Her headlights illuminated dozens of grounded flying saucers clustered in the centre of the compound before coming to rest on the dome they had all recently escaped from. Hundreds of naked men and women staggered out of the shimmering portal in its outer surface and gaped around them. Wicked Tina drove up to them and dived out of the truck.

"What do you want to do?" Bonehead asked, looking at Mia.

Mia watched Wicked Tina embrace someone thin, Tom she assumed, then they both went to the back of the truck and handed out rifles and submachine guns to as many of the survivors as they could before they ran out. Wicked Tina reached back inside for what looked like a large green satchel over-stuffed with something and slung it over her shoulder.

Mia sighed. "Well I guess we go down there and finish this, don't we? One way or another."

Bonehead cracked his knuckles and grinned. "Just what I was thinking. I'll go and get one of them Angel stiffs." He opened the jeep's door, but before he could struggle out Mia grabbed him by the arm and pulled him back. "What's up?" he asked.

Mia climbed over the steering wheel and straddled Bonehead's legs. "Just in case this goes tits up," she said, sliding her fingers around the back of his head.

She pulled him close and their lips met. Bonehead's tongue darted into her mouth. It tasted horrible, like rancid porridge mixed with battery acid, but she just didn't care. His hands found their way inside her leather jacket and up her shirt. They were soft, not rough and calloused like they used to be. Her back arched at their icy cold touch against her bare spine and she felt herself becoming aroused. She ground her hips against his stiffening cock, wanting him so much her heart ached for it. But she knew she would have to break the embrace soon, before they both got carried away and wasted too much time.

"Later," she whispered, climbing over Bonehead and stepping out of the jeep. "We've got shit to do first, remember?"

Bonehead nodded, then followed her out, and together they found another Angel corpse and hauled it onto the bonnet. Mia twisted its arm so the blue disk it held pointed forward, then climbed into the back of the jeep and opened up the hatch in the roof so she could man the machinegun turret. She inspected it to get an idea of how it worked while Bonehead drove into the Angel compound and the soft, rubbery force-field burst around her upper body.

Something very similar to the bullet belt Tanner used to wear trailed out of the left hand side of the gun and into a large wooden box positioned beside it. Like Tanner's belt, the casings were made of brass and linked together with metal clips, but it was a lot longer than any belt she had ever seen before. Mia guessed there must be at least three hundred bullets in that box, and if the other two similar boxes in the back of the jeep contained the same amount it would be enough to wipe out an entire army of Angels.

Wicked Tina stood on Tom's shoulders and opened a portal in one of the domes. Then she jumped down, took a grenade from the green satchel on her shoulder and tossed it into the dome. Everyone dashed away so they wouldn't be caught by the resultant explosion, but no sound came from inside the dome and no smoke billowed out. They looked at each other in confusion for several seconds, and eventually a man stepped forward with a submachine gun and disappeared inside the dome. Everyone waited anxiously until he returned with a wide grin on his flabby face and raised a thumb. The group outside let out a cheer and moved on to the next dome.

Bonehead drove past them slowly and stopped the jeep twenty yards away, while Mia spun the heavy-duty machinegun on the roof from side to side, searching for any sign of Angels rushing out of the other domes to investigate. None came, the domes' surfaces remained solid. She wondered if maybe whatever blocked the sound off from inside the domes would leave them oblivious to everything happening outside until it was too late? That would make it a lot easier to wipe them out if it did.

Another dome portal shimmered, and Wicked Tina tossed another grenade inside. This time an overweight woman stepped forward with a submachine gun to finish off the Aliens inside. She reappeared ten seconds later, her face deathly pale, and leaned against the dome and vomited grey slop on the ground by her feet.

"What is it?" someone asked. "What's wrong?"

The woman shook her head and pointed a shaking finger at the shimmering archway.

"It's not Angels," she said. "It's more people, and I think we just killed them all."

Wicked Tina ducked into the dome to see for herself, and came back out swearing.

"We need to be more careful," she said, "make sure there's just Angels in them first."

Mia thumped a fist down on top of the machinegun. More lives lost, and this time it was their own fault. Wicked Tina was right, they needed to be more careful. For all she knew, the last remnants of humanity could be right here in this Angel compound, and every single life counted if they were going to have any kind of future at all.

A group of naked men and women gathered around another of the domes while Wicked Tina climbed onto the shoulders of Tom and opened up its portal. One of the obese men disappeared inside with his gun raised, under strict orders from Tom not to shoot until he was sure of what was inside.

Seconds later he flew out backwards screaming in agony with an Angel ripping his huge body apart. Everyone cried out at once as dozens more Angels galloped out of the dome on all fours and set upon them.

Mia gripped the machinegun and opened fire on the Angels streaming out of the dome. The roar was deafening, much louder than she expected, and the huge gun juddered in her hands as empty brass casings flew out of the right hand side of it. Angels crumpled before her, yellow and black goo flying out of the back of their heads along with the bullets, but it was already too late to save any of the people who had been standing before the dome. They lay in pieces, their bodies eviscerated by Angel claws.

Mia searched frantically for Wicked Tina, desperate to see her still alive somehow despite all the odds, but there was no sign of her anywhere. Severed Angel arms and legs and bloody clumps of human flesh littered the ground she'd been standing on seconds earlier, and Mia choked back a sob at the thought her best friend must be part of that horrific mess.

But she didn't have time to mourn for long because right then another wave of Angels stampeded through the portal, one after the other, and headed straight at her.

Mia screamed abuse as she fired at them. Men, women and children who had been far enough away to survive the first massacre scattered in all directions, many of them dropping their guns in blind panic.

"Get out of the way!" she yelled at unarmed men and women waddling toward the jeep and blocking her line of shot. She only just managed to stop firing in time to avoid killing any of them.

Meanwhile the seemingly endless stream of Angels bounding out of the dome continued unabated. Dozens of them took the opportunity to find shelter behind the domes, and seconds later their disks hummed and blue lasers reduced fleeing survivors to smouldering ashes.

"Come on, hurry up!" Mia shouted at the small group heading for the jeep.

But they were slowing down, their faces bright red from exertion as they puffed and panted in their unfit state. The Angels were upon the slowest of them in seconds and ripped them to pieces right before Mia's eyes. A morbidly obese and hysterical woman who only just managed to avoid the attack opened the jeep door and tried to climb inside, but couldn't manage it. Mia reached down to help her, but before she could lock hands with the woman an Angel pounced and sliced her open from shoulders to buttocks. The woman fell back screaming as blood poured out of her. The Angel reared up, then stabbed her in the face with one claw and silenced her.

"Drive!" Mia screamed at Bonehead as the Angel turned its attention to her.

Bonehead floored the accelerator and the jeep lurched forward with a jolt. Mia gripped the machinegun with both hands and fired a hail of bullets at the Angels running full pelt toward her, shredding their bodies and pulverising their huge black eyes. A blue laser zipped above her head and she ducked down instinctively as it exploded into the surface of a dome behind her, the sudden ball of flame burning out within seconds and leaving no mark.

Arched portals in the other domes began to shimmer, and Angels poured out of them in all directions. Mia arced her gun across their ranks and mowed down the ones closest to the jeep as it sped past them, but more and more took their place as they bounded over their fallen allies and chased after the jeep. Bullets tore through them and added to the mound of bodies, but still more came, like an unending army of kamikaze locusts determined to get at Mia and silence her gun no matter what the cost.

The jeep lurched savagely to one side and the Angel corpse on the bonnet rolled off. Mia lost her balance and the machinegun spun in her arms as she clung to it, unable to stop firing. Bullets ricocheted off nearby domes and pinged into the air before she managed to right herself.

A young girl Bonehead must have swerved to avoid hitting ran headlong into the path of the marauding Angels heading straight at her. Realising her mistake far too late, she skidded to a halt and gave out a cry of anguish.

"Get down!" Mia yelled.

The girl dived for the ground and Mia aimed the machinegun at the Angels galloping toward her and fired. Dozens of alien bodies juddered and fell in a sticky yellow mess, but there was just too many of them to deal with. The girl must have realised it too, because she rolled onto her back and pushed herself up to a sitting position and raised her hands before her face as one leapt at her with its claws extended.

Mia waited until the Angel sailing through the air was almost upon her, then tilted the machinegun down and blew the top of the girl's head off so she wouldn't feel anything when it tore her apart.

The jeep circled around the grounded Angel ships in the centre of the compound, only just keeping ahead of the mass of Angels as they sped after it, leaving behind a trail of brass bullet casings. Mia's arms ached from the constant hammering of the gun, but she knew she couldn't stop firing until every last one of them was dead.

Then the Angels split into two groups.

Most headed straight for the flying saucers, while the rest continued their pursuit of the jeep.

"Don't let them reach the ships!" someone shouted. Mia couldn't be sure over the roar of gunfire all around her, but it sounded like a woman.

An explosion boomed out in the midst of the Angels rushing for their grounded spacecraft and yellow and white clumps showered down. Rapid-fire gunshot from a group of survivors Mia couldn't see finished off more Angels as they righted themselves from the blast that had bowled them over and resumed their suicidal dash for the ships.

Mia concentrated her fire on the Angels heading for the spaceships too, ignoring the ones still chasing after the jeep. If any of those ships became airborne she knew it would be all over. Bullets wouldn't penetrate them, and there would be no hiding place once the lasers started raining down.

Another blue beam zipped over Mia's shoulder. She ducked and searched for where it came from. All but one of the Angels had broken off their pursuit of the jeep and stood erect, the deadly disks clutched in their outstretched hands. She returned fire and cut one in half with a hail of bullets. The rest scattered away and her bullets pinged off one of the domes as they fled behind it.

Then the Angel chasing after the jeep reared up and pounced with its claws extended, like a cat taking down its prey. Mia cried out and spun the machinegun back to shoot it, but it was already too close and the huge gun's barrel thudded into its body, sending a shockwave down her already exhausted arms. Mia let go of the gun and ducked down into the jeep as the Angel swiped at her. She flattened herself against the rear seat while its claws reached through the access hatch in the roof and tried to get at her. Then it curled its long fingers around the edge of the hatch and pulled itself forward, its legs scrabbling across the rear of the jeep with a sound like fingernails scraping down a blackboard.

"Hold on," Bonehead shouted.

The jeep lurched to one side and the Angel's lower body swung out, but it held its grip on the edge of the hatch and stared down at Mia malevolently through its huge black eye. Its claws scraped against metal as it pulled itself forward and got a whole arm inside the jeep. Mia cowered away from it, wishing she had a hand-gun to shoot it with, and searched desperately for something she could use as a weapon. But all there was inside the jeep was the two boxes of ammunition for the machinegun. The Angel's elongated head squeezed through the hatch. It chirped and screeched at her as another arm found its way into the jeep.

Bonehead zigzagged from side to side and the whole vehicle jolted as he slammed into the side of a dome and scraped against it, but it was already too late to dislodge the Angel from the roof. Within seconds it would be inside with them, ripping them both apart, and there was nothing either of them could do about it.

Mia grabbed the headrest of Bonehead's seat and pulled herself upright. If she was going to die, she would die fighting, not cowering on the floor like a scared rabbit. The Angel screeched at her and swiped with the claws of one hand, but she was just out of its reach and they swished past her face. With a scream of pure hate she balled a fist and darted forward before it could slash at her again and punched it in the eye.

It was harder than she thought it would be, like punching a solid wall, and pain erupted in her knuckles as soon as they slammed into it. But at the same time she felt something crack, and heard the Angel squeal in pain. She drew back her fist and punched it again, feeling it give way a little bit more, and when she punched it for a third time her entire fist broke through the hard surface into something soft and gooey.

The Angel reared up through the hatch with another squeal, its elongated arms flailing. Mia's fist tore out of its eye with a wet plopping sound as she dived out of reach of its deadly claws. The Angel fell back and tumbled off the jeep, still squealing and thrashing its arms while it rolled along the ground. Mia flicked black goo from her hand, wiped it down the leg of her jeans, and retook her position at the machinegun while Bonehead turned the jeep around and headed back toward the Angel ships.

Explosions and gunfire rang out all around her. Blue lasers flew through the air. A small group of men, women and children, naked and covered in shit, cowered against one of the domes while the battle continued around them. A laser hit them and they didn't even have time to scream before they were reduced to ashes. One second they were there, the next they were gone.

Mia spun the machinegun to where the Angel shots had come from just in time to see a tall white figure dive behind one of the domes on the outer reaches of the compound. She ducked back into the jeep, got Bonehead's attention, and pointed.

"Go around that one from the opposite side, there's a bunch of Angels hiding there. But take it slow, we need to surprise them."

Bonehead nodded and raised a thumb. Mia returned to the machinegun while he drove slowly over to the dome she had indicated and navigated the jeep around it in a counter-clockwise direction. There was a slight jolt as the side of the jeep scraped against the force-field at the edge of the compound, then Bonehead corrected his course and took them closer.

Mia gripped the machinegun and braced herself while Bonehead inched the jeep around the circumference of the dome. She waited until all five of the Angels standing there came into view before she opened fire, spinning the gun from side to side with one continuous burst to make sure she got them all before they could react. The Angels squealed as they spun to face the jeep. Three raised their disks to fire back, one last desperate act before their bodies were reduced to a sticky mess.

Bonehead stamped down on the accelerator as the disks hummed. The jeep shot forward and smacked into the Angels, tearing their bullet-riddled bodies in half. Their upper bodies flew over the bonnet and splattered against the jeep's windscreen; their lower bodies crunched beneath its wheels. Bonehead turned on the windscreen wipers and laughed.

But he didn't laugh for long, because seconds later twelve flying saucers shot up into the air and hovered over the compound.

24

Mia screamed in rage as she swung the machinegun up to fire at the cluster of flying saucers hovering overhead. She knew it was pointless, that the bullets would just bounce off them, but there was nothing else she could do.

They had failed.

It was only a matter of time before the Angels wiped out everyone left still alive in the compound, and she would rather go out in a blaze of glory than die whimpering for mercy that would never come.

Other survivors ran for the dome they had been imprisoned in, a mad dash for cover before the Angels started their attack. Maybe they thought a life hanging from tentacles and being force-fed grey swill was better than no life at all.

But Mia didn't share that thought, and the way Bonehead stopped the jeep and just sat behind the wheel to gaze up through the windscreen she doubted he would either.

"Come on, you bastards!" she screamed above the roar of the machinegun juddering in her arms. "What are you waiting for?"

Then they were gone.

One second the Angel ships hovered ominously over the compound, the next they sped off north at an incredible speed. She stared at them as they receded into the distance, then turned to Bonehead, who had climbed out of the jeep and stood beside it to watch the flying saucers go. He looked up at Mia and shrugged.

"That's a good thing, right?"

Mia stared down at him open-mouthed, then looked back up at the sky. She couldn't believe what had just happened, and expected the Angels to swing back for an airstrike at any second. Why would they just leave like that when they had the upper hand? It didn't make any sense.

"I don't know," she said. "Maybe. For now, anyway."

"I reckon we should get going, then, while we can," Bonehead said. "To that place in Northumberland you were going on about before."

Mia nodded. "Yeah, you're right. Let's get the hell out of here."

She thought about Wicked Tina and a painful lump grew in her throat. Then there was Fat Brenda, who seemed to have just vanished. Most likely she was dead too, and Mia and Bonehead were the only two still standing. The last remnants of Satan's Bastards, the only ones left alive to carry the name forward into the future.

Naked figures peered out from their hiding places and stepped gingerly between the remains of countless human and Angel corpses littering the compound to gather around the truck parked outside the dome they had been held in. Mia counted them. Of the hundreds who had left the dome earlier in the night, barely a dozen remained.

Then she remembered the second dome people had been housed in. Surely they couldn't all have been killed by the grenade Wicked Tina tossed inside? If the layout was the same as the first, and they were packed as tightly together, there was a good chance at least some of them would have survived the blast. But would they have time to free them all before the Angels returned? Would it even be possible without Wicked Tina's dagger? Fire didn't seem to affect those tentacles, but maybe a blast of bullets would sever them?

Bonehead got back in the jeep and drove over to the truck, while Mia remained behind the machinegun on the roof in case they came across any stray Angels along the way. More human survivors came out of hiding as they passed by, and followed the jeep on foot. Nineteen in total, five of them children. Mia studied the ashen faces of each adult in turn, hoping Wicked Tina or Fat Brenda might be among the women, but she didn't recognise any of them. Then she spotted Tom leaving one of the domes, and called out to him.

"Is Tina with you?"

Tears were streaming down Tom's face, and Mia's heart sank. But then he nodded and pointed at the shimmering portal of the dome he had recently left. The remains of an Angel corpse had been placed there to hold it open.

Mia climbed through the hatch onto the jeep's roof and

jumped down from it before Bonehead had chance to bring it to a halt. She dashed over to the dome and ran inside, bounding over the Angel corpse in one stride. Could it be true? Was Wicked Tina really still alive in there?

It was the dome that had housed the other humans, and the stench of cooked flesh hit her straight away and made her retch. Burnt remains lay everywhere she looked, the grenade blast leaving behind a crater of charred flesh. White tentacles, untouched by the explosion, hung down from the roof of the dome. Several of them still held up stray limbs that had been blown off in the blast. It was also eerily silent, devoid of the moans of anguished survivors she had hoped to hear.

"Tina, where are you?" Mia yelled.

"Over here, honey," Wicked Tina said from somewhere to Mia's right.

"Did any of them survive?"

"You'd better come and see for yourself."

Wicked Tina's voice was hoarse and croaky, filled with emotion, and Mia feared the worst. So many lives wasted, when they were so close to being rescued. She hoped Wicked Tina didn't blame herself too much as she made her way over to her, noticing for the first time the limbs hanging from tentacles were legs, not arms. She pondered what that might mean as she stepped over burnt torsos and clumps of blackened flesh.

Then she saw the first of the intact bodies at the edge of the grenade's blast radius and stood still as she gaped at them. They were suspended upside down by their feet, their limp arms hanging down below their heads, their fingers trailing several inches from the ground. Their bodies were riddled with bullet holes, but that wasn't what had killed them.

Their throats had been cut, and a huge pool of blood coated the ground beneath them.

"Jesus," Bonehead said, "what the hell is this?"

Mia startled and spun toward him. With his soft, bare feet she hadn't heard him follow her into the dome.

"I don't know," she said. "I've never seen anything like it before."

"I have." Bonehead sniffed, then hacked up and spat on the ground. "Only it weren't people, it were pigs. And I really hope that isn't what this is for all our sakes."

Mia's hand shot to her mouth. She fought down her

revulsion as Bonehead prised apart two of the suspended bodies and squeezed his way between them. Could that really be what this was, some kind of alien abattoir? She shivered involuntarily at the thought. If whatever it was Wicked Tina had found was worse than this, she wasn't sure she wanted to see it. But she followed Bonehead through several rows of cold, dead flesh toward the right hand side of the dome anyway, where she found Wicked Tina kneeling in a huge pool of blood and sobbing into her hands. Bonehead crouched behind her, rubbing her shoulders.

"Tina? Are you okay? Look, we need to go, yeah? There's nothing we can do here. The Angels might be—"

Then she saw the tattoos on the breasts of the huge naked figure suspended before Wicked Tina. Even upside down and flopping over the woman's face, there was no mistaking those words.

Property of Dirk, Satan's Bastards. Hands off.

Fat Brenda's throat had been cut so deep it had almost sliced her head clean off and only a few stringy tendons still held it in place as her hair trailed in the pool of blood beneath her. Her stomach, an unnatural greyish blue in colour, was a mass of deep jagged gashes, but there was no blood left in her body to pour from them.

Other bodies suspended around her, both men and women, hung in the same butchered condition. Some had been sliced open, their internal organs removed. Others were missing their heads.

Mia crouched down and stared into Fat Brenda's upside-down face while Bonehead reached up with Wicked Tina's dagger to cut through the tentacles around her ankles. Her mouth and eyes were wide open. Her fists, dangling inches from the ground, were still clenched as if she'd fought her captors all the way through the ordeal.

Fat Brenda's body fell and splashed cold blood over Mia's face. Her head rolled to one side, twisting the tendons anchoring it to her torso. Mia reached out and closed her eyes and mouth before wiping the blood and tears from her own face.

The woman had been a pain to live with ever since that day they returned from the supply run to find the rest of Satan's Bastards incinerated, and Mia still hated the way she'd kidnapped her away from Little Bonehead and the Brownies to bring her here. But for all her faults, Mia still loved Fat Brenda like a sister. She didn't deserve to die like that. Didn't deserve to be slaughtered and strung up like an animal.

Nobody did.

"Let's get her into the jeep," Bonehead said, placing a hand on Mia's shoulder. "We'll give her a proper Satan's Bastards funeral when we get to that new place of yours."

Mia gripped Bonehead's hand and pulled herself upright. She nodded, then wiped her nose on the back of her hand. Wicked Tina got hold of Fat Brenda's wrists while Bonehead grabbed her feet. They tried to drag her between them, but she was just too heavy. Even with Mia's help, they couldn't budge her. Bonehead puffed and panted when they gave up, his face bright red.

"I'll go and get some help," Wicked Tina said.

She returned several minutes later with Tom and two of the other survivors who still looked reasonably fit. Along with Wicked Tina, they took a limb each and with a lot of straining they managed to drag Fat Brenda through the rows of corpses while Bonehead held them apart. Her head rolled from side to side, scraping along the hard dome flooring, and Mia worried it might come off.

Once they entered the clearing caused by the grenade blast and had a bit more space to move around in, they lifted Fat Brenda from the ground by her hands and feet. Her head flopped down and dangled between her shoulders, swinging from side to side as they carried her.

Mia couldn't watch any more. She ran out of the dome ahead of them, sobbing. She kicked the Angel corpse beside the shimmering portal in the head, then stamped her boot down on it until it cracked open and yellow and black goo spurted out. But it still wasn't enough. She stamped its arms and legs flat, then kicked its elongated body until her boot went straight through it. Then she found another Angel corpse to take out her anger on. And another. And another. Tears ran down her cheeks as she kicked and stamped. Children and adults alike gaped at her in horror, but she didn't stop. Seeing Wicked Tina, Tom and the other two survivors heft Fat Brenda into the back of the jeep made her need for retribution even more acute. She rushed over to another Angel and used her fists like hammers as she set about obliterating its eye.

"Mia," Bonehead said softly. He grabbed her arm mid-blow when she took no notice. "Mia, come on."

"Get off me!" Mia shouted, and wrenched away from him. She shot up and ran to another Angel and stamped on its upturned eye. It crunched and her boot squelched down into its head, sending greyish black fluid spurting up her legs.

Bonehead reached out for her again. "Mia, they're all dead. You're just wasting your time, we need to go while we still can. Before they come back."

"He's right, honey," Wicked Tina said. Mia turned to face her. Her arms were filled with Angel disks clutched to her breasts, all of them with fingers still attached. "They've probably gone for reinforcements from France or somewhere like that."

"France is south," Tom said as he tossed blood-spattered rifles into the back of the truck.

"You what?"

"The Angels went north, France is the opposite way."

"Yeah well, whatever. France, Spain, bloody Timbuktu, it makes no difference, does it? They'll still be coming back with thousands more of the bastards and we don't want to be anywhere near here when they do."

Tom ushered the survivors into the back of the truck while Wicked Tina continued collecting the blue disks.

"What do you want all those for?" Mia asked. "We only need a couple to get the vehicles out."

Wicked Tina shrugged. "Sooner or later the Angels will find us." She dropped the disks in the back of the truck and slammed the door. "If we can work out how to fire those things we'll have a better chance of fighting back."

"You make it sound easy."

Wicked Tina picked up another disk and rammed it into the truck's radiator grille. "Nothing's going to be easy, honey. But that doesn't mean we have to just give up. We kicked their arses today, we can do it again next time."

Tom climbed into the passenger seat while Wicked Tina lifted the bonnet and started the engine with the blade of her dagger before sliding in beside him. She revved the engine and ground it into gear, then pulled forward. The wheels crunched over Angel remains as she drove away.

"You okay?" Bonehead asked.

Mia stared up at the empty sky. "They're going to kill us for this, aren't they? They'll find us wherever we go, then they'll kill us."

"Maybe, maybe not. I guess we'll just have to wait and see. So anyway, this place of yours. There any bike shops on the way? Only if I'm going to die I'd rather not do it on four wheels like some boring citizen."

Mia looked at Bonehead and couldn't help smiling. "I'm sure we could find one. Come on, let's go."

25

Mia couldn't believe how fast Little Bonehead was growing. It seemed only yesterday she'd pulled him out of Diana's corpse, yet now here he was, three years old and full of energy. He ran over to her and raised his arms to be picked up. Mia leaned to one side on her Triumph Tiger and lifted him by his armpits. He spread his legs so she could sit him on the petrol tank between her thighs.

"Vroom, vroom," he said, reaching forward for the belt Mia had attached to the handlebars for him. He held it like the reins of a horse and shook it up and down. "Giddy up, mummy!"

Mia strapped a pair of swimming goggles over his head to guard his eyes from swarms of flies and revved the engine. Little Bonehead whooped in delight as the bike pulled forward across the car park next to the gift shop and onto the main road.

Down by the river Mia could hear the crack of an Angel disk and the sizzle of its blue beam hitting the water. She hoped they would never need to use them, but it was good that Tom had finally managed to figure out how they worked. Soon he would start teaching the others how to do it, then they could at least defend themselves when the Angels came for them. Maybe they would even penetrate the hull of the flying saucers and blow them out of the sky.

Their small community had grown over the years as small pockets of survivors joined them, bringing along new skills and new ideas. An area of woodland had been cleared to grow potatoes and carrots, peas and cabbages. Chickens and goats provided fresh eggs and milk, as well as meat in the winter months. But Mia never ate any of them, she stuck to a vegetable diet. Every time an animal was slaughtered and hung up to drain its blood she couldn't help thinking about Fat Brenda and those other poor wretches in the second dome. How killing animals for food was no different to what the Angels had been doing to humans.

Self sufficiency was hard work, but it meant they didn't need to rely on scavenging from the dead cities to survive. The only thing they couldn't create themselves was petrol. The tanker in the car park was almost empty, so they would need to start looking for a new one soon, otherwise it would be back to siphoning cars again and that would mean returning to the cities of the dead. Something she wasn't looking forward to at all.

Mia knew she would need to tell Little Bonehead about the Angels and what they had done to the world one day. But it had been so long since she had seen any of their flying saucers, for now she was content to let him just enjoy being a child. And to give him the carefree childhood she never had for herself.

"Faster, mummy, faster!" Little Bonehead shouted.

Mia obliged. She twisted the throttle and the bike roared down the empty road.

AFTERWORD

Thanks for getting this far, I hope you enjoyed reading it as much as I enjoyed writing it. If you can spare the time I would appreciate a review on Amazon or Goodreads, or a quick mention on Twitter, Facebook or anywhere else you think it might do some good. You don't need to write a huge essay, just a few words is fine. Doing this not only gives me a warm fuzzy feeling inside and encourages me to continue writing, it will also help other like-minded readers find something they might enjoy.

If you want to contact me about anything at all you can do so at marcus.blakeston@gmail.com or through Facebook or Goodreads. To keep up to date with new releases, along with the occasional free short story, be sure to follow my blog:

https://marcusblakeston.wordpress.com